A Convergence
of Crows

A Johanna Kincaid Mystery

Anneka Lowrie

Stormview Mountain Press
14 N. Reamstown Rd. #44
Reamstown, PA 17567

STORMVIEW MOUNTAIN PRESS

Stormview Mountain Press
14 N. Reamstown Rd. #44
Reamstown, PA 17567

Literary Praise for A Convergence of Crows

Johanna Kincaid Mystery Series: Book One

A band of strong, capable women determined to take down a child sex trafficking ring with the aid of First Nations and other mystical wisdom is a powerful combination in this important story. Lowrie's sweeping natural imagery gives space for readers to process difficult subject matter. While sex trafficking is an oft-explored topic, a seldom celebrated, fierce female presence lights up this book—an antidote to its brutal truths. The infusion of spirituality and its intersection with the natural world provides an impactful additional layer of meaning. Lowrie's characters are vibrant and easy for readers to connect to, despite populating an uncommon, strikingly realized setting. Their backgrounds are fully examined and nicely inform the events unfolding in the present. ~ **Booklife Prize Critic's Review**

This debut novel interlaces a murder mystery, injustices to indigenous people, violence against women, and misuses of power--all suffused with a mystical overlay of spirituality and nature. Johanna Kincaid, retired psychologist and budding Shaman, uses her several skills and friendships to unpack crime, while challenging readers to confront a range of contemporary social issues. Marked by lucid prose and fast paced action, this novel is the first of a series. Look forward to journeying with Johanna along future mysterious ways. – **Louise A. DeSantis Deutsch, Professor Emerita, Dept of Language &**

Literature, Cape Cod Community College W. Barnstable, MA

What sets A Convergence of Crows apart is its fusion of psychological intensity with a mystical twist. The narrative keeps readers on the edge of their seats, unraveling a complex tapestry of secrets and revelations. Fans of the Joe Leaphorn Series by Tony Hillerman are sure to find a kindred experience in the intricate twists and turns of Johanna Kincaid's mysteries. This mystery series is a must-read for aficionados of psychological thrillers seeking a narrative that skillfully blends the visceral with the mystical. – **Emilee Jackson Reviews, Instagram**

I enjoyed the way Anneka Lowrie weaves together the story of Johanna Kincaid's journey into shamanic training and her ability to help a victim of human trafficking. Lowrie explores the horrific underworld of high ranking, privileged desire, and the difficulty punishing crimes against indigenous people. Don't miss this psychological thriller with a shamanic twist! – **5 Star Amazon Review, Barbara Stein**

Trigger Alert

Please be aware this story contains scenes that may be disturbing or cause emotional triggering. It is written with deepest respect for those who have suffered at the hands of perpetrators.

Violence proliferates in silence.

Break the silence.

The Red Ribbon Skirt Society on Facebook

Make a Donation Go Fund Me at

https://bit.ly/RedRibbonSkirt

"Dedicated to awareness and education about the epidemic of missing and murdered indigenous women, children and two-spirit people."

A portion of the profit of the sales of this book will be donated to the Red Ribbon Skirt Society

The clothesline Project

http://www.theclotheslineproject.org

"58,000 soldiers died in the Vietnam war. During that same period of time, 51,000 women were killed mostly by men who supposedly loved them. In the summer of 1990, that statistic became the catalyst for a coalition of women's groups on Cape Cod, Massachusetts to consciously develop a program that would educate, break the silence and bear witness to one issue - violence against women."

Constance

Remembering the day we used our voices
to name the women and children
murdered that year by domestic violence at the
Take Back the Night Rally
The Green
Hyannis, Massachusetts

Find the Missing and the Murdered
Speak their Truth
Say their Names
Hold their Light

Contents

Prologue

S *he crouched on the ground beneath a stand of oak trees. She watched intently. She saw the woman move inside the dwelling down below. The gardens glowed in the golden red glimmer of a setting quarter moon. It was still dark enough to hunt. Hunting is what she did best. She never lost her prey. She could smell their scent in the footprints they left behind.*

Her golden eyes blinked as the light from the rising sun rose silently, on wings of cool, fresh air. Dawn cast a soft crystalline pink hue over the hillside, illuminating tree limbs with muted white edges. As the liquid moon faded into bright rims of light, the sky adorned itself in a pale blue robe the color of robin's eggs. She was a patient and cautious hunter. Worthiness was everything.

Living on a mountain top isn't easy, thought Johanna. She poured a cup of steaming coffee and sat down in a brocaded chair by the cabin window. Up here, GPS coordinates, not roads or names, determine location. N41^ 27.190 W 77^49.388 in the wilds, at Cross Fork. Solitude, peace, ruggedness, and hardship of off-grid living created a blend of freedom and determination.

This, she remembered, as she sipped her coffee, was the reason she and Scott had built their solar farmhouse in this very place. From the ocean, an ancient land had swelled, buckled and gradually rose eighteen hundred feet into the sky. A hillside overlooking a valley and the mountain ridges of Elk Run, Pennsylvania, had become their home. Living on the summit of a mountain is a strange experience, she mused, for those whose sense of safety involves streets, buildings and the comfort of human activities.

The sharp call of morning birds, robins, crows, and doves pierced her thoughts. These sounds were her clock these days, the signal to roll out her yoga mat and greet the day with sun salutation, triangle, tree and warrior poses. Both she and the earth were in a mountain pose, together. She smiled and placed her coffee cup in the sink.

She stepped out onto the wooded deck by the kitchen, rolled out her mat, faced east and the rising sun. Her days began with a prayer and ended with the chanting of stars.

Before she worked in the garden and the kitchen, she dwelled in meditation. Turning inward, she thought, I am the union of peace and emptiness. I take refuge in the Buddha, the Dharma and the Sangha. This meant she dedicated her practice to becoming an awakened one, who followed a path of truth and had joined the community of meditators. Now her Sangha was elk, deer and eagles instead of other meditators.

The surrounding earth, the gardens and the flowers sat in the same perpetual meditation. She entered their sentient space on fingers of light as the day emerged. Just be here, she thought. Just notice and loosen the mind.

For twenty-five years, her work as a clinical psychologist had required her to be absolutely present in the face of traumas and suffering, grief and loss, pain and triumphs. She guided her clients in journeys of healing and self-discovery. She had loved her work. She had given all of her focus to her work. She had nearly lost the love of her life because she failed to develop the balance she taught her clients.

Her work, now, was the gardens and the farm. Scott had woken, stirring about the cabin and getting ready for his day. For six years, he had been singularly devoted to shaping the hillside into a sustainable, resilient natural habitat. He had built the solar cabin, created a terraced slope of swales for the gardens. He had dug a pond and planted sea-berry and elderberry. He was happy. He was happy with her and their life together. It had not always been so.

Today she planned to plant potatoes and tomorrow, the sunflowers and the gladiola bulbs. She would bake cranberry muffins with almond flour. These days her hours were measured in projects, weeding, clouds and rain instead of fifty-minute increments and filing insurance claims. She knew Scott was happiest with his hands in soil, measuring and building. Now he built his own designs on his own land rather than those of others. He had found his peace and he was highly protective of it.

Scott was an early riser and out the door as the sun rose. He liked to walk the land. He liked to feel he was at work before anyone else. It helped him focus his mind on the tasks of the day. More often than not, he picked flowers from the garden, ripened fruit or gathered pine cones to leave on the kitchen table.

Johanna loved working in the garden. It was hard and physically demanding but she countered the forward bending and crouching with yoga poses throughout the day. Barefoot, she stood daily on thyme and purslane covered stepping-stones that wound pathways through the vegetable beds. Truly dwelling in a meditative balance between striving and allowing, between smelling the scent of roses and knocking beetles off the leaves of their food.

When she and Scott first found this property she had called her friend, Angelique Boudreau, to help her listen to the land. To ask the land if it wanted to be used in the ways she and her husband wanted to shape it.

Angelique was an indigenous born woman whose gifts with land-speak were legendary among her people. Some would have called her a shaman, a term that would cause her to shake her head with an amused expression and roll her dark, sparkling eyes. She sat on two tribal councils and was actively involved in her community.

As they stood barefoot on the untouched hillside, Johanna had held a compass in her hand. Angelique had stood beside her listening to their plans of a creating a resilient, sustainable solar powered farm. "It likes off grid," she murmured. "No electric poles or man made radiation."

Angelique was standing on a flat rock. "Hmm," she said. "Find 0 degrees east on your compass."

Johanna held the device out in front of her and began to slowly turn. They had been facing the west and as she turned to the left, it began to wildly change its digital location from southwest to south. She moved as slowly as she could as the numbers counted down to zero degrees east. "There," Johanna said.

"Don't move," said Angelique softly. She took a stone from her bag and placed in front of Johanna's bare toes. "Now slowly turn until you find zero degrees north."

Again Johanna turned to her left. The compass was very sensitive and she had to stand perfectly still as she turned her hand to find true north. She nodded her head gently. Angelique placed the last stone in front of Johanna's toes.

Then came the laugh. Angelique's notoriously hardy laughter spilled out across the hillside. It started as a giggle that sounded like raindrops on a rooftop then cascaded like a waterfall plunging down the side of a cliff. To say it was infectious was an understatement. It was unmatchable by any other human being.

"Look at the cross-hairs of your compass, Netuksq. You are standing in the center of a great medicine wheel. The Eastern door is the stone on your right; you must have a ceremony place and entrance on this side of your dwelling. Behind you is the South, the place where you must create your gardens. By your left foot is the West and you must place your bedroom on this side of the house. Before you is the North, the place of spirit. Things must come and go on this side of the house."

"Aren't we always standing in the middle of a medicine wheel, as far as compasses go," Johanna had asked, thinking this was nothing special.

"Yes, our hearts, wherever we stand, are the center of a great medicine wheel. Wherever we are standing, is a place called Here. Within us is the place of healing. Look above you. Father Sky. Look below at your feet, Mother Earth. Feel the wind on your face. Your sisters. Smell the trees. Your brothers. We just need to know their direction if we are to ask for their blessings."

She now stood in mountain pose, arms extended to the sky. Then, slowly raised her foot and locked it against her knee in tree pose. Beauty to your right, remembered Johanna in her ceremony that morning. Beauty to your left. Beauty before you. Beauty behind you. Above you. Below you. Within you. Yes, her Sangha was vast. It was time to work in the gardens.

She watched the woman reenter the dwelling. Her nightly ritual of stalking ended in a morning ceremony of light, colors, movement and the grace of dancing winds. Like any adept predator, she withdrew to the coolness of the forest.

She doesn't know it yet, thought the creature, but that woman has some very sharp claws.

True North Asks A Favor

May is a deceptive month. The winter ground may seem soft, but frost persists in the mountains until later in the month. Many of her plants were still in greenhouses on Scott's raised beds. Starting the peas and lettuces in her greenhouse and transplanting their tender shoots by the end of May seemed safest. Johanna planted according to the Almanac, and there were eight types of vegetables in her garden.

The hardiest vegetables had been planted in the ground last month; broccoli, cauliflower, cabbages, and radish. Other plantings waited under the cold frames for their debut in the garden. Tomatoes and sweet peppers grew in one long tray with cucumbers, squashes and melons on another.

Johanna was a short woman whose compact stature held a strength and flexibility that was deceptive in a woman her age. Despite being almost sixty, her dedication to yoga, kayaking, and healthy living made her look much younger. Her formerly dark blonde hair was now streaked with silver strands and she wore it long. Today she pulled back into a ponytail.

She paused to finish her coffee as Scott walked in the door.

"There are mountain lion tracks in the mud by the upper pond," he said, hanging up his jacket.

Living on a mountain meant sharing your world with wild souls who wandered through on business of their own. The trick was to live respectfully without encroaching on their ancient rights to the land. Johanna recalled their initial spring on the mountain when Scott used an excavator to shape the land swales for the future gardens. It was late afternoon when a herd of elk silently glided past and headed into the woods. They followed migration lines traveling along ancestral paths of ghost elk.

Scott had shut off the noisy machine as they both watched as the graceful creatures moved across the land. Johanna knew he was marking their route in his mind so the landscape of their travel would remain undisturbed by his plans to shape and contour the planting areas.

Two reasons: respect and avoiding garden repairs. Six years later, the path of the elk was a well-worn trail of grass and dirt that wound around and between the various gardens, shrubs, and sheds. Creature and human alike now traveled it.

Neither one of them had ever seen a mountain lion in the Pennsylvania Wilds. The postmaster in town and the woman who owned the general store mentioned a lot of wildlife in the area, but they had only heard stories of mountain lions. No one they knew had ever actually seen one.

Johanna kissed her husband as she left to set the potatoes in the ground. Her morning of planting and baking beckoned her. She welcomed the thought of hiking by the falls.

Much later, she removed her dirt encrusted garden sandals and headed for the outdoor shower. It was a refreshing ritual to rinse her body under the bright warmth of the sun. Clear mountain water poured through her hair and cleansed the dirt and sweat from her body. A red-tailed hawk flew over the shower. She closed her eyes. A mourning dove called out for its mate. She breathed in the scent of sweet clover that wafted on a warm morning breeze. There was peace on her mountain and she drank it like sweet water.

Still later, she pulled a tray of muffins from the propane stove's oven. They soon filled the kitchen with the fragrance of warm almonds. Setting the tray on a stone tile, she turned to the door. Time to alert Scott for lunch and the preparation for an afternoon hike.

Two hours later, they closed the doors of the Subaru and tightened the laces on their hiking sneakers. Adjusting backpacks with water bottles and snacks, they headed out along the Kettle Creek trail. They held hands as they walked into the woods. Sharing glances of intimate appreciation, they walked almost as silently as elk along the creek bed path.

Scott was a tall man, muscular and fit, with striking blue eyes and perennially bronze skin from years of working in the building industry. The forests, mountains and rivers were like a cathedral to him, in which the choir was the sound of hawks overhead and a sermon, the purity of a blue heron taking flight over a lake. Yet he carried a loaded pistol tucked under his belt and a can of bear mace in his pack. Serene, yet wild - it was a place of predator and prey.

A root strewn trail curved along the flow of the creek and the elevation was slight at this point. The sound of the water gurgling and splashing its way along the rocky creek was soothing. The air moving across the water bathed them with a refreshing coolness. Silently they walked, each taking in the sights and sounds of the woods. Crows called to one another. A hawk soared above. The path became steeper and the sound of water rushing over the rocks became louder as the elevation rose.

Their hands dropped away as their arms were now needed to create the swing of balance and motion. They wound their way through boulders and flat rock. Apart but together. It had not always been that way.

Several years ago, they had formed a distance that resulted in a separation. It started with impatience and careless words. Johanna had little time for their relationship due to long work hours. His lack of success frustrated and disappointed Scott. His mood was often curt and dismissive. While Johanna was supportive of his distress, she deliberately focused on satisfying the demands of the health spa, where she provided counseling to wealthy patrons. He saw her as detached, overworked and disinterested in his struggle.

For a while, they remained together, but apart. The bonds of mutual respect that had been the strength of their relationship had become worn and jagged. They called this period of their lives "the separation." But it was more than that. They had divorced. Currently, only a few close friends knew they had never legally remarried.

Together, they weathered a storm that had crushed other couples beyond repair. They had come to agree, the key to remaining together was to never believe their love was so rock solid it was unbreakable. The key to a shared happiness was to remember how fragile love could be, if not embraced with more courage than confidence. They had done bad things to one another. They had been careless and mean to one another.

They were not out of the woods yet, as Scott put it. They were still wandering together, as other couples, sometimes lost and sometimes found.

Hiking together strengthened their bond like a protective seal. Hiking was something they both enjoyed. They discovered they could each deepen their sense of solitude while immersed in the intimate presence of one another. Like the herd mind of deer and elk that traveled together through the forest as one, they felt their souls entwine on the paths they walked. They hiked because they loved to move through a natural world without shaping or changing it. The ability to feed their relationship, both intimacy and adventure, provided a natural mending of their individual brokenness. Hiking allowed them to become an integral part of the natural world in all its momentary wholeness.

As they neared the falls, the water became more turbulent; the air flowing across their bodies became cooler and the path steeper as it led up to the cascade pool. They leaned into the land as they climbed higher. They rounded a bend in the path and came to a sheer rock overhang.

This precarious curve was a familiar place for them. On their first hike to the falls, Johanna almost gave up at this very place. The path wound around a crumbled, narrow overhang with an abrupt edge that plunged over the roaring waters of the creek.

"I can't do this, Scott," she had said, "go on ahead. I will wait for you back at the fallen tree." The simplicity of that moment had defined them as no other incident could have done. "I am not going on without you," he had said loudly, over the sound of the water below. "You can do this." He went around the rock first, then held out his arm. His muscles glistened with mist from the turbulence below.

"I've got you," he said.

So she did. Putting out her arm and holding on to his, she swung out and around the overhang. She knew committing to the traverse meant returning the same way and doing it again. The hike to the falls was a continual re-commitment to their union.

The falls were a wild place. It was a place where deer, elk, and other creatures of the forest came to drink in the pool below. It was as much water for the soul as for the body. The falls crashed through holes in the mountain, not above it.

The pool below was a cistern of liquid mountain. It was a place of wordless replenishment. It was a sacred place for two people who had nearly lost what was most important to them. Each other.

By the time they drove back to the top of Elk Run, the sun was lowering in the sky. As they rounded the corner by the barn, they could see a red pickup truck in their driveway and a tall, long-haired woman sitting in an Adirondack chair on their porch.

"It's Angelique," said Johanna.

"I have to check the upper pond again," Scott responded. "That will give you two a private moment."

He waved to the woman on the porch as he dropped Johanna off, then parked the Subaru by the barn.

The two women embraced.

"Would you like some iced black birch tea?"

"But of course," Angelique replied and settled back in the porch chair.

A few moments later, Johanna returned with two glasses of iced tea. The two women sipped the herbal drink and looked up at the sky. Angelique was wearing faded blue jeans with a plain red T-shirt beneath a hand embroidered blue denim jacket. She crossed her long, slender legs.

"Did you get my message?" Angelique asked.

"Nope. No bats in my dreams lately," responded Johanna.

Many years ago, when they were on a semester break from graduate school, Johanna saw a little black bird that suddenly flew erratically through a dream she was having. Angelique left a message on her voice mail the next day.

"That was no strangely flying little black bird," Angelique had stated when they finally connected. "It was a bat. My spirit teacher, or rather, one of them. I was given the ability to walk into other people's dreams. It is a gift I use very carefully." "Not a bat this time," said her friend. "Don't worry, you'll find it. This one is looking for a medicine person to advise. I sent her on you."

Johanna nodded. This was not the first, nor would it be the last of the enigmatic worlds Angelique often shared with her.

"I need your help," she stated. "Someone with your particular gifts."

Angelique and Johanna had worked together for many years. They knew each other very well. No matter what Angelique needed, Johanna would always be willing to assist her.

"I understand," responded Johanna.

Trapping A Wild Soul

A ngelique took out her cell phone and leaned back in the Adirondack chair. She sighed. A troubled look crossed her face as she settled into her story. Depending on the circumstances, she spoke in several distinct tones. People in her culture carefully memorized traditional stories from thousands of repetitions, speaking them with a specific cadence. Her teaching stories often began with the phrase, "your people.." When she told the stories of other nations, the four-legged, the winged, standing ones, her voice always sounded far away. She sang healing stories in a traditional language.

Angelique had taught her that stories are a form of medicine. This was not one of those kinds of stories. This story, Johanna could tell, rocked her friend to her very soul. Johanna became silent, her body very still.

"Early this morning, I was driving along the mountain road. The sun was just up when I came around the curve by the Ice Mine Cut. You know, the place you used to call the rock fall. A compact car had driven off the road, like it just didn't straighten in time from the steep curve. It looked like an accident, so I slowed down."

She took a long sip of her iced tea and slowly continued.

"There was a pickup truck pulled halfway off the road and a man was standing by the driver's side door of the disabled car. I thought he had stopped to help. But he had a gun in his hand. He fired it."

She paused.

"He pointed it at the back seat of the car and that's when he saw me. He holstered his gun and walked quickly to his truck. But I snapped this picture with my cell phone first."

She leaned forward and showed Johanna a photo of a man looking directly at Angelique. As he put his gun in a shoulder holster, the camera froze him in its view. Beside the truck was a car facing the guardrail sideways. When Johanna zoomed in, she could clearly see both license plates and the man's face.

Johanna waited as Angelique leaned back in the chair.

"As he drove away, I ran over to the car. The driver had been shot in the head. A woman. She was clearly dead. There was a blood-spattered child in the back seat, staring ahead blankly. She was alive. I grabbed her out of the back seat and ran back to my truck. I had to get out of there in case he came back. I turned around and drove up the Hyner Run just to get off the main road as soon as I could."

Johanna felt her chest tighten.

Angelique continued.

"I asked the girl if the woman in the car was her mother. She said no. She said, my mother sold me to that lady."

Angelique stopped, words choked off.

"Trafficked…" Johanna whispered.

Her friend nodded.

"We cannot go to the police," said Angelique. "We cannot put this child at further risk. Social services will take her and they will give her back to her mother."

"Who will sell her again. She needs medical attention, Angelique. Who knows what may have already happened to her? How old is she?"

"I would say about ten or eleven years old. Johanna, it has already happened to her. We have seen this before. Too many times."

Angelique was the retired director of an agency that offered shelter, resources and counseling to battered women and survivors of incest and sexual assault. Johanna had worked with her years ago as a staff therapist. They were both mandated reporters for children and elders who had disclosed abuse.

"We have seen how this ends up," continued Angelique. "We have been in courtrooms with children whose lives were ruined, and we have witnessed judges ruling that their parents have a right to see and be with them. These children learn the hard way, never speak of what is happening to them to anyone ever again."

"We can save this one," said Angelique softly.

"There may be a trafficking ring involved. We have to bring in the police."

"You are forgetting, this is no longer about the trafficker. She is dead. A man killed her and wants to kill this child too. If the police are involved, there is no way to assure her safety. You know this as well as I do, Netuksq."

Angelique's use of her special name found its mark in Johanna's heart. "Where is she?"

"She is safe. I cannot tell you unless you promise to help in a certain way. It may be dangerous. It may cost you your clinical license."

"This child has no one," Johanna said. "No one but us. I am in. No matter the cost."

"Thank you, Netuksq. Spirit is in charge here. We need your gifts. Not your spiritual gifts. We need the clinical skills of a white woman, whose assessments count for something in a court of law. Please come with me and witness her medical exam. This is something you have done before at the agency. You have written the notes. You have signed the forms. It is your clinical skills and the respect of your license that we need."

"You can do that at a hospital."

"We can't bring her there. No protection."

"Social services and the police will be called. I get it. But who? How can such an exam be done?"

"A tribal doctor who is also a medicine person has been called. The child is not a member of the tribe, nor was she harmed on tribal lands, so there is no jurisdiction. We can store any evidence at the tribal medical center. Safely. Your witnessing of the exam gives it credence in a US court later if necessary."

"What has this child said about what has happened to her?"

"Nothing. Nothing at all. After she said her mother sold her, she stopped talking completely. "

"Selectively mute?"

"I believe so."

"I will do whatever you think is best, Angelique. Do you need me to go with you now?"

"Yes, if you can. I can take you there and bring you back later when the exam is done."

"Let me tell Scott I need to go with you. He will understand."

The tall woman rose from the Adirondack chair. The wind lifted her hair from her shoulders and spread it like the dark fringes of a dancer's shawl, edged in the golden light of a setting sun.

"Johanna, this child has become a wild soul. We need to trap her spirit, guard it and return it to her when she is safe again."

Johanna nodded. She saw her friend's face darken as a shadow passed over it. She felt Angelique's shock and sadness engulf her own spirit. She could not count the number of times they had fought this same battle.

A half hour later, Angelique drove away with Johanna riding shotgun.

A Place Called Here

The way to Nadine Thunderchild's farm was a series of back roads and switchbacks. It wound around creeks and rivers and passed over a trout stream where anglers waded during the day in the clear mountain runoff waters. One road rose to an elevation of one thousand feet before suddenly becoming a narrow dirt path that twisted its way over a mountaintop. On one side was the steepest ravine without a guardrail Johanna had ever seen. At the bottom, a creek splashed its way through a rugged gorge. On the other side were the stark, blackened rock bones of a mountain.

Angelique's truck climbed slowly in first gear. Fallen trees and slid down boulders littered the sides of the curves. No worries about deer leaping out in front of them here. The mountainside was too steep. They crossed an invisible boundary and drove over the border into New York State.

"So you added taking a child over a state border to our list of crimes?" asked Johanna.

"My people don't see borders the way you folks do. Wherever we are is simply a place called here. Besides, why stop at

misdemeanors when you are on a spree," was her fearless
response.

It was nearly sunset by the time they reached the gate.
Angelique stopped and texted. A few moments later, the gate
swung open. They drove onto an access lane in the fading light.

"A word of caution," Angelique said, "Nadine doesn't care
much for white people. She will likely ignore you."

"I can respect that. Probably never found any reason to trust
us."

Angelique parked her truck by a large barn. "She rescues
off-track thoroughbred horses. The ones that have made as
much money as their owners could get out of them then were
auctioned for horse meat. She re-trains them for a second life."

Johanna winced. "How old are they?"

"I think she gets them when they are seven or eight years old.
Racing is all they know. It looks like the tribal medical doctor
is already here. She has probably done this kind of exam more
times than anyone we know."

They closed the truck doors and walked over to the ranch
house. A tall woman in her forties, lean and muscled, opened
the front door. She was wearing a red flannel shirt and faded
blue jeans with a silver and turquoise concha belt. Her long,
dark hair was bound in a single twisted braid that flowed down
her back like a tumbling waterfall. She stepped back to allow
them entry. Johanna smiled into the woman's expressionless
face.

"Where is she?" asked Angelique quietly.

"In the back bedroom, asleep," responded the woman. "Anita is in the living room."

"Nadine, this is Johanna Kincaid. She is going to help the child get through this."

"Johanna," she continued, "this is Nadine Thunderchild. She owns this farm. This is where the little girl is being kept safe."

Johanna looked up at Nadine, who nodded stiffly, then led them into a spacious room. On one of the walls was a bleached white skull, a horse's head, mounted on a background of soft tan deer hide. Colorfully woven Pendleton wool blankets were draped across the chairs. An older woman with a medical bag sat on a deep leather couch. She stood up.

"Anita McNee. I am happy you have come." She clasped both hands around Johanna's single, offered hand, and held it tightly for a moment. She looked deeply into Johanna's eyes and held her gaze strongly for several moments. To Johanna, it was like gazing into shimmering pools of dark water, wavering in the subdued evening light.

"Anita, this is Johanna Kincaid. She worked for me at the agency years ago. She has done this before, many times. She was a trauma specialist."

"Thank you for doing this, Dr. McNee. For understanding the situation and being willing to do this exam," said Johanna.

The doctor was nearly the same height as Johanna. She wore simple brown slacks and an untucked white dress shirt. Her face was deeply lined with wrinkles crafted by age and sunlight, immeasurably kind and somber. Her taupe colored hair was streaked with gray and silver strands as if streamers of moonlight had been caught and held captive by some gentle force. She was much older than Johanna expected, in her seventies, but still vibrant. Her movements were graceful and gentle, purposeful.

"Call me Anita. I understand it all too well. My people have suffered over much from these types of people. If I can save a child from their abuse and terror, I am happy to do so. I will keep the rape kit in my evidence locker. Sadly, there is not a lot of room. No one comes for the evidence. No one cares to. This kit will be safe among all the others."

Nadine stepped back into the kitchen. "I will make some supper and tea. You are vegetarian, Johanna? I have some corn-cakes and blueberries."

"Oh thank you, it's good of you."

"I am grateful you have come to help," she stated flatly, then turned away. Angelique followed the woman into the kitchen.

"I have given the child a sedative, she will be cooperative through the exam and will not remember anything," said Anita kindly.

'What sedative," asked Johanna, "a hypnotic? I can make sure I give her some comforting words at the end. She will hear everything we say, whether she consciously remembers or not."

Anita nodded.

They entered a darkened room at the end of the hallway. A small figure lay on a massage table under white sheets that had been set up in the center of the room. Anita approached the child, took her blood pressure and pulse. A plastic bag with blood stained wipes was on the nightstand by a twin bed in the corner of the room. Anita nodded toward the bag.

"Nadine and Angelique washed the blood from her face and neck and put the wipes in an evidence bag. They could not bear to leave her in that condition until I arrived. We can add that into the notes."

She opened her medical bag and removed two pairs of surgical gloves, handing a pair to Johanna. She removed a micro digital recorder and placed in on a small table next to the makeshift exam table. Lastly, she removed evidence bags and the specialized exam kit.

"Ready," she asked.

Johanna nodded, picking up a note pad and pen with her nitrile-covered fingers.

Anita took scissors from her bag, holding them up deftly as if they were precision surgical tools. She pressed the play button on the digital recorder.

In a flat, professionally detached voice, she stated the date, the location, the need for anonymity and the names and professions of the two examiners present.

"The female child, a Jane Doe, is approximately ten to twelve years of age and is sedated for the duration of this examination due to apparent trauma and the intrusive nature of the exam itself. She is of a dark complexion, possibly bi-racial, with short, curly black hair. The witness to the attempted murder of this child, Angelique Boudreau, stated she found the child in the back seat of a Toyota Camry splattered with blood from the shooting of the driver, a woman whose identity is not known to the witness or these examiners. The witness upon rescuing this child from the possible return of the attacker washed the blood from the child's face and placed the wipes in a plastic bag. I am transferring those wipes at this time into an evidence bag."

Anita looked at Johanna, who made a note confirming she witnessed the transference of evidence as described.

Anita then took the scissors and cut off the child's clothes, starting at the hem of both legs, pulling the fabric away from the girl's body gently. She cut the waistbands on both sides. Then she proceeded to cut the side hems of the t-shirt the girl was wearing, noting it was dirty and smeared with droplets of blood spatter as well.

"I am placing the victim's clothing in an evidence bag," she said. Johanna added this to her witness note.

"The victim is lying on her back. She appears thin and malnourished. Her body is bruised at the level of inner thighs, legs and her arms, biceps and triceps having multiple hematoma, some dark, black and blue suggesting injury within the past 24 hours, others faded and healing. I will photograph them for the record as I proceed."

Anita continued, "I am beginning at her feet, scraping under her toe nails. For the record, this girl has had an expensive pedicure with bright red nail polish on her toes. The scrapings are being collected and marked in an evidence bag." Before proceeding to carefully trim the child's toenails, she gave Johanna a piercing look.

Johanna made her notation, and Anita nodded. She then continued to examine the condition of the child's legs, which were thin and dirty. She stopped to take photos of the child's feet, legs, and thighs, which were covered with evenly spaced bruises. Anita put the camera down and retrieved a small forensic ruler. She measured the distances between the bruises. On one thigh there were three bruises of different size. On the other thigh, there were four, nearly identical in width and circumference. On the calves of both legs were similarly sized bruises. Anita called out the measurements.

"For the record, I believe these bruises to be caused by someone holding her down. It takes a lot of pressure to leave marks like this." Anita's mouth formed a tight line as if she wanted to bite off the very sound of her own words.

She retrieved her smallest speculum and prepared to proceed with a vaginal exam, but stopped suddenly. She took the camera and photographed the child's vulva area, then got a forensic tweezer.

"What's this?" she said. "A detached pubic hair. This child has not reached puberty. She has no secondary sex characteristics yet. This may belong to her attacker. I am placing this hair in an evidence bag."

Johanna looked up, then swiftly wrote her witness note.

Anita completed the vaginal exam, taking fluid swabs and noting the condition of the girl's vaginal area. "She is bruised, scarred, hymen not intact, recent tissue tear consistent with forced intercourse. This child has been raped multiple times over a period of weeks or months."

She placed samples in the evidence bag and took more photos before moving up to her chest area. Beginning with the left side, Anita scraped under the girl's fingernails, noting again a bright red nail polish that was neither worn nor chipped. She clipped her nails and added the glistening, half moon shaped, red nail shavings into an evidence bag.

"There is a similar pattern of bruising on her upper arms, around biceps and triceps, indicating she was likely held down or forcibly shaken by her perpetrator."

Anita took smaller scissors from her bag and snipped a short length of hair from the child's head, noting it on the evidence bag. She then took a comb and slowly, methodically, combed the girl's hair. She then placed the comb and hairs caught on its tines in another evidence bag, noting these were not attached to the child's head. Upon analysis, they would either match the other samples or not.

"Can you help me turn her over?"

Johanna put down her notepad and helped Anita gently turn over the little girl's limp body. Anita placed a pillow under her head and turned her face to the right. She continued her exam, noting there did not appear to be any bruising or injuries to this side of her body.

Anita palpated the girl's neck gently when her fingers touched a small raised bump on the back of her shoulder. The bump offered resistance to the pressure of the examiner's touch. It slid beneath the skin.

"What on earth is this?" she murmured, then paused the digital recorder. "It's hard and right under the surface of her skin. I am going to remove it."

Anita placed a sterile surgical field drape around the object embedded in the child's shoulder, removed a scalpel from its hygienic packaging. She cut expertly through the layers of skin and pulled out a small, cylindrical object. She dropped it on a sterile pad and proceeded to seal the wound with tissue sealant, hygienic surgical, super glue. She applied a topical antibiotic and bandaged the wound.

"Is that what I think it is?" whispered Johanna.

"It appears to be a pet microchip," responded Anita, looking directly at Johanna.

The doctor's warm dark eyes had turned cold. A fierceness passed across her unwavering gaze; a wild, ancestral anger that froze Johanna to her very bones.

"Tagged like an animal, a possession," Johanna gasped.

"Indeed, and how very typical of a colonizer to tag a human being as his property," continued Anita.

Johanna held up an evidence bag and saw fire dancing in the eyes of this medicine woman.

"Let that be his fatal mistake," Johanna said, her lowered voice sounded like a piece of steel tempered to the shattering point. "He may believe he owns her, but we may have his name on this device. We own him now."

Anita dropped the microchip in the bag, restarted the recorder and in a steel edged voice of her own, described her findings, location and surgical removal of a foreign object. Johanna documented the placement of the object into the evidence bag.

As she completed her examination, Anita stated she had drawn blood when she sedated the child and would run toxin screens, sexually transmitted disease, and other lab tests for general health conditions. "I am now taking a salivary sample," she said as she swabbed the inside of the child's mouth. She placed the swab in a tube and capped it. She took the final evidence bag and place the tube inside it. She stopped the recording tape after stating her conclusions.

"A DNA test,' she said to Johanna. "This will determine her ancestry in case she has been a sex slave so long she no longer remembers her origins."

They completed the examination by signing the evidence log with their names. The attending doctor's and mental health counselor's licenses bore the legitimacy of their professional capacities as witnesses. They gently dressed the girl in one of Nadine's long flannel shirts.

Johanna leaned over the sleeping child. She placed her hand over the girl's small hand. She felt her healing energy spin. She felt the heat as it transferred from her to the child.

"Sleep, little one. You are safe with us. You are cared for. You will heal. You will become strong. You are protected. When you wake, you will feel safe and comforted."

When she looked up, Anita was gazing at her with a softness in her deeply lined face. In that moment, Johanna saw the young woman Anita had once been. She saw a girl just as vulnerable as the child sleeping beside them. A girl who used her gifts and skills to become a doctor of medicine and whose powerful spirit focused on keeping her people whole.

Together, they moved the little girl into the twin bed and covered her with warm blankets before leaving the room.

Four Crows

Though the hour was late, the farm table was generously spread with food. Steam rose from freshly grilled steaks. A bowl of salad greens and cucumbers, along with corn cakes and blueberries, graced the center of the table. A pitcher of iced tea stood beside colorful plates and napkins.

Nadine entered the room with a bowl of fruit as Angelique stood up from the couch. They looked at Anita and Johanna.

"It's as we feared," Anita said. "She has suffered beyond imagination. She may never speak again. She should never be interviewed by law enforcement."

Nadine put the bowl on the table. "She can stay here indefinitely. She needs both time and space to heal."

"This is not an investigation," said Johanna. "Even though we have followed protocol and documented everything possible, we do not plan to alert the authorities. We need to keep her safe."

"I was able to obtain a pubic hair that cannot belong to the victim," stated Anita. "Ordinarily, it would be used to determine the DNA of her last attacker. In addition to that, I discovered she had a microchip embedded in her shoulder. I removed it."

"Wait," said Angelique, "if it is a GPS tracker, her trafficker can find her here, right?"

"No," replied Nadine. "They do not usually have a GPS in them. Just the name and address of the pet owner." Her voice caught in her throat at her words. Her face flushed with anger. She swiftly walked back into the kitchen.

Johanna looked down at the floor. Angelique walked over to Anita. "What can be done?" she asked. "This girl can't be the only one in a sex trafficking ring. How can we find out if there are more without putting her at risk?"

"Right now," Anita said thoughtfully, "she is a Jane Doe. She is in a safe house. She has been provided medical attention and I will be running tests. What if I speak to my tribal police about this situation? First, they will ask if she was found on tribal territory. Technically, I could say yes because the farm is on tribal-held property. Nadine is a tribal member."

"There is too much to lose if it goes wrong," said Angelique. "Can you prepare the lab reports, hold the exam kit in storage? The DNA on the pubic hair won't degrade, will it?"

Nadine returned to the living room. "Please eat. We don't have to decide right now. I can call my equine veterinarian in the morning. She has a microchip scanner."

They sat at the table and ate somberly.

"Please consider staying the night Angelique, Johanna," asked Nadine as they finished their meal. "Our little deer may need you both in the morning."

Johanna nodded.

"I have to leave," said Anita, "but I will 'accidentally' forget to put the microchip bag in my exam collection kit. Nadine, please call me tomorrow after your veterinarian has scanned it. I will come back and get it."

"Make sure you feed her very small meals. Her stomach has likely shrunk," she added.

Nadine gently smiled for the first time since Johanna had arrived.

Angelique nodded. "It's a start, a name and address, hopefully. Right now, this child's safety and healing is our priority."

Johanna pushed her plate to the side. "Thank you for a delicious meal, Nadine. But it just breaks my heart to see what this child has endured. It's a horror. It's crucial to find a way to identify her rapists and her exploiter.

As the four women stood up from the table, Johanna said, "I see four crows standing."

Nadine raised her eyebrows.

"In the Celtic tradition," Johanna said, "we have a story about crows. If you see one crow standing in a field, pay attention. If you see two crows, it means someone is talking behind someone else's back. If you see three crows, they are talking about you. If you see four crows standing in a field, it means they are plotting against you. I see four crows that are going to take down a sex trafficking ring."

"Now you know why I love this woman so much," said Angelique softly.

"The Lakota people have a tradition about crows too," said Anita. "They say their sacred laws are wrapped in crow feathers. These laws come from Spirit and supersede any ideas created by mankind."

"Well, we know how the dominant culture's laws work for indigenous people," responded Nadine. "What do more than four crows mean?"

"A murder, of course," replied Angelique.

Johanna accompanied Anita as she checked on her patient. The child was breathing softly, regularly. Her blood pressure and heart rate were normal. "She will sleep now, hopefully through the night. Keep her door open and a light on in the hallway, in case she wakes up and doesn't know where she is. The sedative has already worn off, but she is probably exhausted."

"Thank you Johanna," said the elder woman, taking her hand again within her own. "Your involvement will make a very big difference in this child's recovery." She looked into the younger woman's eyes and saw a darkness in her soul. In her vision, she felt something smothered, a terrible sadness and a tree with a violent scar on its side. Then nothing. This woman has a dark secret that even my gift cannot pierce, she thought. To casual eyes she appears vulnerable, but she is strong beyond measure. The Medicine Woman sensed the presence of ancestral energy around Johanna. Then she released her hands.

After Anita drove away, Angelique and Johanna accompanied Nadine to the barn. The horses were in their stalls for the night. Nadine gave treats to each one, speaking softly to them as their heads poked over the stall door. She explained, "I ask a lot of them during the day. They work very hard. Some days are successful, others are not. At the end of the day, I honor them for being magnificent creatures.

Angelique rubbed a horse named Rampage behind the ears, his calm demeanor seemingly belying his name. Johanna stood quietly aside; breathing in the pungent smells of the barn, the sound of nickers as each horse anticipated a treat.

At the last stall, Nadine paused, holding her hand held out. The horse balked and didn't come to the stall door. He stamped and stood against the back of the stall, refusing her offer.

"He is my latest rescue," she said. "His last race was a month ago. When I got him, you could see his ribs. Their metabolism is so high when they race; it takes a lot of time before they put on weight. He still thinks he is going to run."

"What's his name?" asked Angelique, looking into the stall.

"Stable Ticket," Nadine replied. "No, really," she said at Angelique's expression. "I give them barn names when they have found their new life. It becomes their true name. The one the Creators chose for them, the one that reveals their true nature," she said for Johanna's benefit. "Stable Ticket is this horse's registry name. I haven't ridden him yet. He is not ready. He is somewhat aggressive. It will take a while. I was told he was very fast. A million dollar horse."

"How old is he?" asked Johanna, coming to stand by the stall door.

"Eight. That's a little old for a rescue horse. They raced him a year longer than normal. He was that good."

The three women looked at the horse. He was sixteen hands tall, thin, and had a black coat, darker than most thoroughbreds. He looked back at them from his left side, turning his ears turned back. He stomped, snorted, and shook his mane. Nadine tossed the treat in his feed bucket. He immediately put his head in the bucket and ate it.

Nadine laughed.

"It's a nightly ritual. I give out the treats. He ignores me, but he wants it. He will come around. They all do. That is why Spirit sends the special ones to me."

She looked at Johanna carefully. "Our little deer will come around. This is a healing place. I know this."

"If you need my help, Nadine, I will give you my cell number. Text me any time, day or night."

"I will," she replied. "I will call my vet after breakfast tomorrow. I will tell her we found a pet microchip in the trailer after picking up my last rescue. No animal, just the chip. Can I text you both with the information?"

"Yes, of course," replied Angelique. "I still use my secure app from the agency. Let's link up through that and use it to communicate exclusively. Let's use our agency's underground procedure, Johanna. Do you remember it?"

"Yes. I agree we can't take any chances. "

"I will fill you in, Nadine."

Nadine nodded, shutting off the barn lights and securing the doors. She stopped at an alarm system and armed the front gate, while Johanna texted Scott to let him know she would be home in the morning.

He returned her message with one of his own; *"you are the woman of my dreams. Be safe."* She blushed.

In the morning, Nadine and Angelique were in the kitchen making a pancake breakfast. Johanna sat on the leather couch as the little girl entered the living room.

Johanna smiled. The child looked at her guardedly.

"Nadine is making breakfast. You must be very hungry."

The child nodded.

As they sat around the table, Nadine offered her a small serving of silver dollar sized pancakes. "Yours are special," she said. "There are chocolate chips in them. My daughter loved them that way when she was your age."

She then introduced Angelique and Johanna as her new aunties. The girl looked up from her meal, a splash of melted chocolate on her chin. She smiled tentatively.

"After breakfast, child, would you like to help me feed the horses?"

She nodded and returned to her pancakes. *Laney had told her sometimes they won't hurt you as bad if you keep smiling at them.*

A Simple Request

Angelique dropped Johanna off at Elk Run and waved to Scott, who was drinking coffee on the front steps as she drove away. She had sent Johanna's phone a secure text image of the two vehicles at Ice Mine Cut. When they zoomed the photo, the make and tag numbers of both vehicles were clearly visible.

Johanna's daughter was a county sheriff dispatcher in a neighboring town. She would call her daughter to see if the driver's name could be determined. She and Angelique decided to tell her that a man driving the truck with those tags had nearly run Johanna off the road.

Scott greeted Johanna with a hug, pulled her hands to his chest and held them tightly. She could feel the strong beat of his heart beneath her palms.

"The good ones never truly get to retire, do they?" he said.

Johanna smiled at Scott, feeling love and gratitude well up in her own heart. We take these gifts of devotion and relationship for granted, she thought. So many people in the world never experience such depth of trust. Theirs was hard won and had suffered through despair and loss. She thought of the child at

Nadine's farm and the anguish of being sold into a life of horror and abuse.

Professionally, she knew the possibility of healing was very slim. It would be a difficult road. And yet, she herself had seen abused people make that journey and arrive at a life of purpose, meaning, and a firmly held belief in the sanctity of their own lives.

Johanna turned to her greenhouse and surveyed plantings she could put in the ground that afternoon. She was not too far off her planting schedule. In the back, on shelves with bright sunlight, were the seedlings of her medicinal herb garden. The area outside the kitchen was to be expanded from plots of cooking herbs to include medicinals this year.

She needed to prepare the growing space first, much as she had done in the past for her clients engaging in the process of therapeutic healing. The soil to be used was prepared and honored, permissions were asked of the land and offerings made.

She had carefully designed her private practice office with a tea center, fountains with splashing water, and soft spa music to greet those who waited to be seen. In the inner office, there were deep chairs with soft fabric in a room with maroon and tan painted walls, soft lamp lighting and abstract art on the walls.

The back of the inner office had a massage bed for bodywork and hypnosis. There were built-in shelves lined with books about psychology, philosophy, myths, and religions. Books written by Carlos Castaneda were tucked beside those of Carl Jung. The Tibetan Book of the Dead and The Applied Psychophysiology of Biofeedback placed beside trauma treatment manuals.

Healing space was specific to its purpose. She would need a small garden with fountains, walkways and hanging flowers. She had plenty of time to create a live growing, healing garden.

Johanna dug a row of holes and splashed some water into the bottoms. Then, taking sets of green peppers, she blessed each one and hummed a chant as she planted them in the ground. She savored the texture and smells of the dirt as she covered each planting, a caress of healing energy for each plant that would grow to feed their bodies.

Memories filled her mind. She saw images of clients she worked with at The Glen in the energy healing room. In a managed care setting, such as her private practice, healing energy was not a covered expense. Her energy medicine work was classified as clinical hypnosis. But in the employ of the integrative medicine department of The Glen, a prestigious international spa, she was able to expand her repertoire to include energy healing and shamanic journey-work.

A familiar face came into her mind. It was one of her repeat clients of many years at the spa health center, before the trauma of her own broken marriage had occurred. Jayne was an architect and Feng Shui practitioner with a deep-seated sadness. They had worked together using journeys and exploratory hypnosis to identify her feelings of abandonment. Jayne had designed Johanna's private clinical office many years ago.

The image was powerful. This was one of Johanna's many gifts. She had the ability to see images in her mind that were either premonitions or offered clarity in confusing situations. Why Jayne, why now, she wondered.

Standing up, Johanna set aside her trowel and watering can. She looked at the long rows of plantings. She wiped her hands on her jeans and drank cool water from her jug. Time to make a phone call, she thought. As she entered the kitchen, Scott was snacking on an almond muffin and gazing out the window, lost in thought.

She walked over to him and kissed the back of his neck. He reached up and took her hand.

"I missed you," he said softly.

"I missed you too."

This was not said in an accusatory way. It was a simple statement of fact they had grown used to admitting to one another. After coming so close to losing any possibility of a relationship, they had decided that blunt honesty was the foundation of the only authentic relationship they could ever really have with one another. Sometimes that got very edgy.

"Do you think there is anyone else in the world who has a love like ours?" he asked.

"It's impossible to know," she responded. "It takes a lot of courage to be this vulnerable to another person."

He nodded.

"How are the elderberry and sea-berry coming along?"

"Good," he responded. The solar farm was a regenerative design. Circular planting zones with swales that used the natural elevation of the mountain to contour its terrain surrounded it. The inner circle was closest to the farmhouse. It contained all the vegetable gardens for personal food consumption.

As the zones moved away from the farmhouse, they contained more perennial plantings and larger, taller crops. The upper swales contained the slowest growing trees and bushes and provided their cash and trade crops, sea-berry, elderberry, and apple. The upper pond that gravity fed and irrigated the lower zones was at the top elevation by the pine forest.

Johanna went into the study and closed the door. She took out her cell phone and called her daughter, Kaye.

"Hi, Mom," Kaye responded.

After a few moments of their traditional check-ins and family discussion, Johanna stated, "I have a professional request for you." She texted her daughter the Pennsylvania tag numbers that were on the truck's back plate. "*It's a white Chevy Silverado pickup. The driver nearly drove me off the road the other night. Is it possible to get the owner's name?*"

"Why don't you report the aggressive driver to your local police department? You know I can't look that up for a citizen, not even you," she responded, changing from her normally humorous tone to her dispatcher's sharp, no-nonsense voice.

"Yes, but around here, there are influential people. I don't want to make a complaint that backfires on your father and I."

"Yes, and I don't want to lose my job. I can't help you. Tell the police department your dilemma."

"We haven't lived here long enough to know the town politics."

"Understand. Maybe you want to leave it alone for a while. If it happens again, report it."

"Thanks honey. Good advice. Do you want to come up the mountain for dinner some weekend? We'd love to have you."

"That would be great, Mom. Let me run it by Ron and get back to you."

They ended the call.

This investigation just hit a dead end, she thought. Hopefully, Nadine got a better response from her vet.

It would be at least six weeks before food could harvested from the garden. She had stored onions, turnips, white and sweet potatoes in the root cellar. Dinner that evening would be a vegetable casserole she could put together quickly and bake in their propane oven. The peace she felt in her heart would be translated into freshly baked artisan bread and a meal that strengthened her relationship with the man she loved. A memory flowed around the edges of her thoughts. After Jayne's husband had died, she had begun a new relationship. Her partner was an ex-cop turned detective. Any information she shared would be bound by confidentiality.

"It might just work," she thought as she placed a secure text message to Angelique. She needed higher approval before trying to obtain information using a private detective.

A few hours later, she received an answering text. A "thumbs up" emoji.

The Circle Widens

Johanna's cell phone contact list contained many of her past clients, including those she saw at The Glen. Jayne's information came up quickly. She placed a call to Jayne's business number and connected with her voice mail.

"Hi Jayne. Johanna Kincaid here. I was wondering if I could book a consultation with you as soon as it's convenient. Give me a call. I hope all is well!"

She put her cell phone in her back pocket. Scott had already left. He had to go to a lumber company in the valley and would not be returning until later that day. She decided to hike the property.

Hiking helped to clear her mind. It was a meditation in motion and she enjoyed both the physicality and the clarity. She decided to walk up the hills to the upper pond. Putting on her backpack and sneakers, she left the farmhouse and walked up the main driveway to the north of the property.

At the top were outbuildings. This is where they processed the apples, elderberry and sea-berry making ciders and two kinds of medicinal syrups. Scott had decided it was easier than maple sugaring when they were developing a cash crop. There was a storage barn where they labeled and kept an inventory of goods. During the production months in the fall, the area was busy with processing and UPS pickups.

This part of the solar farm was Scott's endeavor. He pruned and cared for the trees and bushes that formed the outer perimeter of the property. Her domain was the inner gardens and farm kitchen. There were three ponds, aptly named upper, middle, and lower. The lower pond was both garden irrigation and a swimming hole.

Today, she wanted to hike a trail that Scott had blazed. She had walked it just once with him before he painted the trail markers on the pines that wound to the top of the outlook. It took about half an hour to reach the vista that overlooked the surrounding mountains and creek below.

She found the bench that he had built from wide pine planks. Mist curled around the base of Elk Run, along the winding creek. She sat.

Her cell phone buzzed.

It was a message from Nadine on the secure text line they shared with Angelique. *The scanner picked up the name of a kennel and address in Pennsylvania. Little Mountain Saluki Breeding Kennel and the words, Ruby Tuesday. Advise.*

A dog kennel. Johanna felt a tide of anger rise in her body. A child with a dog breeder's kennel chip implanted in her like an animal to be sold to the highest bidder.

The cell phone buzzed again. Angelique. *I am on it.*

Johanna texted her response. *Waiting to hear back from a friend who has connections for discreet investigations. Will update.*

Nadine's response: "*All is well here. Will wait to hear from you both.*"

A check-mark appeared from Angelique.

Johanna replied the same.

She looked out across the landscape of mountain, forest, sky and creek. The beauty of the world she saw below was not tainted by acts of intentional cruelty such as humans wrought. It was true there was violence in the circle of living creatures. Predators and prey existed in all species. But that was a matter of survival, not cruelty for the sheer purpose of doing harm. Her own kind was capable of heinous acts not imagined by the natural world.

When she first met Angelique so many years ago, fellow students would often ask her what her native name was. Her friend would smile and respond, "you can call me Angelique." They did not know what that question cost her emotionally. It was a constant reminder of ancestral oppression and annihilation.

"My true name is a gift," she had once told Johanna. "It's a gift with a terrible price. When I went to the white school, my mother had to register me with an English name. They would not accept my native name. That was fine with her. My father was French and Abenaki so the name Boudreau followed me.

My mother wrote the word 'Angelique' on my registration form because it was my French grandmother's name. Not mine."

"My mother explained why she did this," her friend had continued. "She told me they won't be able to pronounce your name, so it will sound all broken to the Creators. They will want to know what it means in their own language. Then they will twist it around because they will not understand it. Be careful who you give your true name to."

Johanna not only knew Angelique's true name, she knew what it meant. "She Who Laughs" had spoken the name by which the Creators knew her; in the language They Themselves had given her people. Johanna honored her friend's decision to never be called that name, other than in ceremony.

"It's a native person's decision to share their name. If they give you an English name," she taught, "accept it and use it. That is how you can honor them. If they give you a translation, accept it. If they give you their name in the language of their people, honor that gift by learning how to say it properly."

"Your people have a peculiar way of showing respect," Angelique once told her. "You make people feel they have to earn it. We regard everyone as gifts from the Creators the moment we meet them. Then all our actions are intentionally ones of honoring. Nothing can express this more than how we respond to their name."

Johanna remembered the day Angelique had first called her "Netuksq." Sister. It was the same day she learned the first act of oppression against a person was to take away their language.

Conquerors colonized by removing the language of the people, the sound of spoken words given to them by the Creators. Ideas were lost, as words no longer meant what they were supposed to mean. Children's voices could no longer wrap their minds in the wisdom and knowledge of their people.

"Our people guard our language, passing it down only in ceremonies and private settings. We are told not to speak it in front of white people. You can't steal what you cannot find. Learn the language of the colonizers so you appear compliant and do not share the sound of your world with them. So far it's worked well," Angelique had said softly, "now we are allowed tribal schools in which we teach our language and ways of life to our children."

Her thoughts turned to the rescued child. They did not know her name, perhaps the child herself didn't. Selectively mute or traumatically shocked into silence, her lack of speaking would be honored by Nadine and Anita. The child could recover in her own way rather than being forced to speak by means of psychological crowbars.

Sometimes, Johanna thought, psychotherapy was an act of violence we inflict upon people. If anything could heal the torment and torture of what had been done to this child, the earth alone contained its secrets. She, herself, had no real answers.

By the time she had hiked down to the lower pond, the sun was lowering in the sky. She poured a cool glass of birch bark herbal iced tea and sat in an Adirondack chair to wait for Scott's return.

Her cell phone buzzed. Jayne was returning her call. She answered.

Oatmeal Cookies

Nadine mixed the oatmeal, flour and honey into a batter while the child chopped apples and carrots into small pieces. The oven was heating. She suspected this was the girl's first cooking lesson. Making oatmeal cookie treats for the horses held a special appeal.

Each morning by six, Nadine fed the horses and turned them out in the paddocks. She now had a new and willing helper. Her only communication was a nod or a shaking of her head to indicate yes or no. She eagerly put on boots and gloves to accompany Nadine to the barn both morning and night. She helped feed the horses; carefully noting which horse received which particular feed bucket. This is how Nadine determined the girl knew how to read.

Today's cooking lesson came about because of a special relationship that was growing between Stable Ticket and the girl. Nadine had begun to lunge him daily. This was the practice of attaching a long rope to his halter and encouraging him to run in ever-widening circles around her as she fed out the line. Newly retired from the track, he only bent one way. Due to the nature of racing long tracks that turned to the left, these horses were often stiff. They had the ability to bend in that direction, but hardly any flexibility to the right at all.

Lunging both helped subdue the high energy of a racer while slowly building back their ability to move and build muscle strength. Lunging in both directions was one of the building blocks of returning these magnificent creatures to a healthy life. Later she would put him under saddle and begin the serpentines that would build more stamina and flexibility. Whether he would become an eventer, a jumper, a dressage or trail horse was yet to be discovered.

The child led all the horses out to the paddocks except the newest rescue. Stable Ticket was unpredictable at this point. A stall pacer, he often turned his back and refused his nightly treat. Nadine knew he must have been mishandled at the tracks. Transitioning to a new form of performance training was often difficult for these animals that only knew how to race.

This horse exhibited classic symptoms of abuse. He often refused his food and shied away from human touch. Unused to the peaceful quiet of her stables, he would suddenly react to the sound of loud crunching as other horses ate from their grain buckets. His behavior was much more intense than simply coming down from his former life at the tracks. She had seen him remove himself from new situations a number of times. This was how abused horses protected themselves from unexpected events.

Last night, before taking the horses into the barn, Nadine saw the child approach Stable Ticket, who was on the far side of his paddock. The pail of treats were hung over her wrist. She leaned against the fence.

She took out a treat and held it up over the fence rail. He slowly approached her. Head held down, with his ears forward, he walked over to the fence in her direction. She held out the cookie. Nadine held her breath.

The horse took it gently from the child's outstretched fingers. She turned around and saw Nadine watching. Slowly, the girl turned around and walked away from the fence. Nadine held up her hand.

"Stop there, look back at him, over your left shoulder."

She did. The horse stood by the fence, watching her.

"Now, turn away. Walk away toward me and don't look back."

She did. The racehorse followed her along the paddock fence line as far as he could and whinnied to her. Nadine smiled. It was time to expand both her new rescues' abilities to respond to unfamiliar cues.

And so the cooking lessons began along with riding lessons. Rampage was good at equitation and was learning trot poles. He would be a good horse for the child. Nadine figured they would learn together. Stable Ticket was in training to recover his lost agility. He would soon learn to walk, trot, and canter when asked. Rampage would teach the girl how to ask. She would find her seat.

They mixed the carrots and apples with the batter, then formed small rolled balls of cookie dough. Placed on trays,

Nadine put the cookies in the oven. "Who says we can't eat them too?"

The girl smiled. Her lovely, liquid dark eyes sparkled in her beautiful brown face.

Trust comes from consistency, thought Nadine. This was how she forged relationships with rescued racehorses. When they knew they were safe, fed, and able to find a purpose for being, they would do anything she asked of them to the best of their ability. Their individual gifts would be revealed. Presenting nightly cookie treats was the way she honored the power, skill and endurance of these incredible creatures.

She recognized Stable Ticket had likely been abused by his handlers. Having never seen a child at the tracks, he responded easily to this young girl. Fearing grown handlers and grooms, he was able to respond naturally to a human he sensed was not capable of harming him. Both vulnerable, both abused and exploited, Nadine knew she was seeing the work of Spirit forging healing beyond any human level of skill.

This young girl, whose childhood had been stolen, responded to the simplest of kindnesses. Making meals together, baths, and hair braiding had become routine. When asked if she wanted to learn to ride, the little girl had nodded her head vigorously.

The lessons would not be easy. Nadine demanded a great deal from her riders as well. Their safety depended on learning the right handling, the right postures, and hand signals. They needed to learn how to ask for the trot, the post and the canter yet not demand or pull on the horse's mouth. A relationship of respect and reciprocity had to develop.

Nadine ran a tight training school. The futures of these horses, formerly destined for death, depended on her unique skills and gifts. It was not in her to fail them.

Her phone suddenly chirped, signaling an incoming text. It was Sam Red Deer at the gate, delivering a truckload of hay. She pressed the key on her cell application to open the gate.

"The hay truck is here," she said to the girl. "Take the cookies out when the timer goes off and I will be right back when we're done."

Nadine grabbed her leather gloves by the door and headed out to greet the truck. The girl watched cautiously from the window. She flinched as one of the horses in the corral spooked and dashed across the ring, bucking and leaping as the truck backed up to the barn.

She watched a muscular, dark-skinned man with tattooed arms get out of the truck and climb onto its flatbed. He wore his long hair pulled back in a ponytail and it whipped around as he threw down the bales of hay. Nadine leaned out of the barn loft above and lowered a hook. The man attached it to twine that wrapped around the hay bale and Nadine hauled it up into the loft.

He was an older native man dressed in worn jeans and a torn flannel shirt. His face was creased with deep wrinkles, worn into his craggy face through years of exposure to the sun and wind. There was a quiet power in the decisiveness of his movements.

He threw down a few more bales from the truck before helping Nadine hoist them.

The horse neighed and rushed the gate. He pulled up suddenly, shook his mane, then slowly trotted away.

"Something tricky about that one, Nadine," he observed. "He has a second sense."

Nadine knew what he meant. The horse was wily; a little something more than a horse. He was a dark bay with one white sock and a white blaze on his forehead. His former racing name was Good Alchemy and he had proved himself to be a good jumper. He had just received a new name, Merlin. It fit.

When Nadine returned to the kitchen, the tray of cookie treats was on top of the stove, but the child was not there. She was not in the bedroom. She called out to her, but there was no response. She walked out onto the porch and called the child again. There was only the sound of a light breeze in the trees. She walked toward the paddocks and the back entrance to the barn.

As she walked by the stalls, she heard Willow nicker softly. When she looked over the horse's stall door, she saw the child cringing against the wooden sidewall, silently crying. Nadine entered the stall and sat down in the wood shavings beside her. She gathered the girl into her arms and held her tightly. Willow nudged the girl's head.

Whiskey Dick

L ights were flashing from every conceivable direction. Trooper Trace Helberg raised a hand to her forehead, as if that alone could ward off the inevitable migraine. The train crossing lights were flashing bright red, along with the strobe lights of emergency vehicles and her state police SUV. Mercifully, the flashes were not synced. The intermittent strobe effect was like a bad light show at a rock concert or missile launch tracers in a nighttime battle zone. Like Afghanistan.

She winced.

The mangled white pickup truck had been hit broadside on the tracks by the two am freight train on the Norfolk Southern line. The local Emporium police reported a suicide on the rail tracks. What a way to go, she thought. She keyed the mike.

"Dispatch, can you run a Pennsylvania tag? We got a train wreck here."

"Go ahead," a calm male voice returned over the state police band radio.

"White, Chevy Silverado. Tango, Zulu, Echo 2310."

She waited. The EMS team was still extracting the body using the Jaws of Life. It was going to be a long night. The train engineer was being treated for shock. Other than the driver of the Silverado, no one else had been injured or killed. The train engine had sustained some minor damage and the Norfolk Southern crash team was on its way. Until then, freight wasn't moving on this track. The rail line was down.

"Dispatch to Helberg.."

"Go ahead," she stated.

"Valid registration to one Thomas Dresden, out of Philadelphia. Not stolen. Need an address?"

"Waiting on the driver's license to confirm," responded Trace. "They are extracting the body now."

She surveyed the crash scene. At this hour, there were no commuters and the area traffic was light. This was the only benefit to a rural assignment, she thought, as bystander interference was always a pain in the ass. A few delivery trucks were being detoured around the scene by the local police while the fire department stood by. The flashing lights illuminated the glowing green bands on the emergency team's black jackets, producing an illusion of gleaming banners intermittently darting in all directions.

The state-contracted wrecker had just arrived, its flashing yellow running lights adding to the bright bursts of color. The road flares disturbed her brain the most, provoking painful memories that continually sat at the edges of her mind.

She sipped her coffee. Caffeine might allay the incoming headache. It was bad. Skunk piss. Whoever made this stuff needs to be shot, she thought. It should be a crime to burn coffee.

She saw some movement down on the tracks as the gurney was being wheeled over the embankment toward the meat wagon. She could see the zipped black body bag in the harsh flickering light. An officer walked toward her and handed her a plastic evidence bag containing a blood-soaked wallet. She sighed.

"He's off to the coroner," reported the officer. "Poor bastard. Wish I knew what makes people do this to themselves. Is anything really that hopeless? A train? Jesus!'

"We don't know that. Things aren't always what they seem, officer. Maybe his truck stalled; maybe he was drunk and passed out. Our investigation is just beginning."

"Yeah, well, I've seen enough in my day to know what happened here." He walked away.

She ran her fingers through her close-cropped red hair. Another jibe, although this one was more subtle than usual. She was a rookie and everyone seemed to know it. Rookie to police work, she thought, but not to life. And certainly not a newbie when it came to all the ways a person could die. She put on nitrile gloves and opened the plastic pouch.

Extracting the Pennsylvania driver license from the wallet, she noted the name, Thomas Dresden, Philadelphia, PA. Inside another fold was a Pennsylvania license to carry firearm permit, a Utah concealed firearm permit and an Arizona concealed weapon permit. All bearing the same name.

She looked up at the twisted and contorted piece of metal that had once been a pickup truck. She held up her hand to stop the wrecker driver from winching it up to the tow bar. Vehicle search. She sighed again. No one has this many firearm permits and no firearms.

Tom Dresden, she thought cynically, had been taken out by the Whiskey Dick midnight train to Buffalo.

Road Trip

Johanna had agreed to meet Jayne at The Glen the first weekend in June. She had booked a two-night stay in the very hotel hosting the spa that had employed her several years ago. As she drove out of the central mountain area and onto the New York Thruway, she pondered how she would approach her unusual request.

A private detective had to maintain confidentiality, but she had made a promise not to reveal the child's location. As far as her part in the situation, she needed to decide just how much she could discuss. The goal was to find out the names of the drivers of both the Silverado and the Camry. If a detective could provide that information, they would have the identities of a trafficker and a murderer. Both of these people were connected to someone who exploited children.

Two identities and a location: Little Mountain, Pennsylvania. A kennel for show dogs that might be a front for child sex trafficking. At some point, she realized, the only way to stop the operation was to involve law enforcement. She knew legal authorities found these activities just as abhorrent as she did.

The only difference was, in her experience, many police officers, lawyers, and doctors were so uncomfortable with it, they couldn't look at it when it stared them in the face. They operated in a domain of emotional denial. They did not believe a child even if they showed clear and recognizable signs of abuse. Their testimonies were invalidated because they were deemed too young to testify. So children with bruises were often sent back to their abusers.

Generally, children displayed behavioral symptoms rather than specific memories or the ability to disclose facts. When abuse and neglect were common daily experiences, a child did not know how to tell someone what was happening to them. They were often aggressive toward other children, because it was the only way they could create a safe distance from others. They had difficulty handling separation from a safe parent and suffered from a number of somatic issues. Even worse, often these children had been threatened, they or their siblings would be killed if they revealed the unspeakable horror they were enduring.

She had seen children draw very specific pictures detailing abuse they could not have possibly imagined unless they experienced it. And yet, because they could not speak about it, investigators and social service workers refused to believe it happened. "Not enough evidence" was a poisonous mantra she had heard way too often. Children were left to fend for themselves against a violent perpetrator who knew their victim had been silenced.

She remembered with a shudder the female sex crime investigator who told her some children were born more sexualized than others when she filed a report after a young child demonstrated tying up her dolls in play therapy and using her fingers to pretend to snap photos in a therapy session. They dismissed that case.

Johanna drove on. Most people would not believe a child they knew was being trafficked. It was always some other child in another town or school. It was hard for some people to believe a child they knew of, taught, or had as a patient was being attacked nightly by a parent, clergy person, a relative or friend of the family. And yet, it was more prevalent than most people knew.

She had learned from clients, not textbooks. Incest survivors spoke of the three am wake up call. They told her about family members who knew what was happening but did not tell anyone for fear of what the abuser would do to them. They spoke of their abuser, forcing them to drink alcohol so they could not physically resist them. They talked about being disbelieved when they tried to tell a teacher what was happening to them. They spoke of being forced to watch child pornography so they would know what was expected of them.

Johanna's clients had grown up and left their abusive families. This meant that the greater part of their adult lives was focused on journeys of recovery. They believed they were not truly free to live their own lives until their abusers were dead. Each person she worked with stated the same thing. Until their abuser died, they believed they could find and harm them again. Sometimes that meant the survivor became a victim by means of suicide in order to end the cycle of predation.

But to be sold into trafficking was to be made utterly invisible. Like the horses Nadine rescued, if these trafficked children were not found and rescued, they would die. They would live short lives of abject misery, unbearable pain, and never experience love or affection. Touch would be a sensation of fear instead of human connection.

Tears slid down Johanna's face as she drove on to the Berkshires. They had to proceed with caution yet remain decisive. They could not put this child at further risk. They could not trust a tainted legal system to protect her.

A few hours later, she checked into the hotel at The Glen and got the keys to her room. The clerk said, "Ms Cullen said to meet them in the Orchid Cafe when you settled in."

The Glen and Spa had changed management in the years since she worked there. There were several restaurants on the hotel grounds. The Orchid Cafe must be one of the new names, thought Johanna.

"Where is the Orchid located?"

"It's in the courtyard by the library."

Johanna brought her luggage to her room and freshened up from the long road trip. She walked across the pavilion toward the library's entrance.

The Glen itself was a gilded age property that included a carriage house, mansion with a large portico and an inner garden courtyard. The stately mansion was constructed of brick and marble in an elaborate French architectural design. It rose three floors and was crested with roof top balustrades. The grounds included forested trails, serene ponds and stone fountains.

They had maintained the library in its original 18th century style, with dark wood paneling, stained glass windows and a central stone fireplace. The Orchid cafe was an alfresco outdoor eatery located within one of the hotel's magnificent flower gardens. Tall pergolas shielded the guests sitting at wrought iron cafe tables. June was a beautiful time of year for open air dining at The Glen.

Jayne saw Johanna as she crossed the slate paved walkway and waved her hand. Beside her sat Marti, dressed in a tailored lavender blouse and slacks. Jayne stood up as Johanna approached the table and hugged Johanna warmly. Marti stood and offered her hand.

Johanna took Marti's hand and looked into her clear, discerning gaze. She remembered Marti from a session at The Glen several years ago, after the murderer she had been investigating had nearly killed her. Marti was a woman of uncompromising integrity, sharp intelligence, and a slight self-consciousness.

They smiled at one another and sat down. The wait staff took their order for appetizers and drinks. Johanna ordered lemonade. She needed all the clarity she could muster when she presented the details.

"I thought we could relax for a bit before we got to business," said Jayne. "Marti will get us take-out and we can hear your story over dinner in our rooms for privacy. Did I ever mention Marti used to be a police officer?"

"I used to be a therapist."

"A pretty good one too, as I remember," laughed Marti.

Plates and Trains

J ohanna opened her side of the connecting door between the two rooms and knocked lightly. The other door opened and Jayne smiled.

"Come on in, Marti, just brought us Mexican food!"

"Did you tell her I'm a vegetarian?"

"Of course. Veggie burrito and taco salad with guacamole and sour cream."

Jayne stepped back and pointed Johanna to the spacious dining area in her luxury suite. It included an attached kitchenette. Johanna's room was a smaller version of the luxury suite, the same bold colors and rich fabric textures without the kitchenette and dining area.

"And the best Mexican street corn I have ever tasted," said Marti as she opened the take-away boxes and distributed the foods with their distinctive smells of cayenne, cumin and chilies into bowls and plates. "If we are going to talk about murder, the least we can do is eat well," she joked.

"Iced tea or wine, dear one," asked Jayne.

"Better make it wine now since murder is on the menu," said Johanna.

"I like her even more," said Marti. "She has gallows humor."

Johanna's cell phone dinged. "Um, I better take this," as she fumbled with the pass-code. "It might be about, uh, the.."

"...case.." finished Marti, as she finished setting out the colorful combinations of steaming food.

"Yes, hi hon," Johanna said. "I am with some friends. It's OK. Yeah sure, it's a good time to talk." *My daughter,* she whispered.

Jayne poured wine into three glasses, setting them on the table, and gave Marti an intimate glance.

"What, he did what?" Johanna gasped. "That's not possible. He had no reason to. Are you absolutely sure?"

Marti sighed and sat down at the table. Jayne looked at Johanna with concern.

Johanna looked stunned, and that was really something. As a therapist, she had mastered the art of a neutral face, even in the midst of traumatic and emotional client outbursts. Her head nodded as she listened to the voice on the other end of the line.

"Thanks for letting me know!"

She hung up the call. "The hit man just got hit by a train!"

Jayne reached over and touched Johanna's leg. "You better start at the beginning, dear."

"Yes. I should." Johanna took a deep breath. Marti pushed the glass of wine toward her with a gentle smile.

"About a week ago, a friend of mine was driving along a road well known for its falling rock zones early in the morning. As she rounded a bend ahead she saw two vehicles, both pulled aside from the lane. One car, she thought, appeared to have had an accident. The driver of the other, a pickup truck, seemed to have stopped to render assistance."

"As my friend pulled over to see if she could help as well, she saw the truck driver fire a gun, killing the driver of the disabled vehicle. He started to point the gun at something in the back seat. That's when he saw my friend's truck."

Johanna paused to take a deep breath and then continued, "he quickly holstered his gun and ran to the driver side of the truck. He drove away, but not before she snapped this photo of him. She went to the Camry and found a little girl, alive, in the back seat."

Johanna revealed the child's story of being sold to the woman who had been driving the Camry. She shared the cell phone photo that Angelique had texted her. She zoomed in so Marti could see the tags on both vehicles and the face of the man with a gun in his hand. "We have models, makes and colors of both vehicles, both Pennsylvania tags."

"Now,' she said, 'we apparently only need the name of the Camry driver. That was what my daughter was calling about. She is a dispatcher for another county. I asked her about the driver of the Silverado a few days ago, but of course she couldn't look it up for me. "

Marti nodded. "Of course not."

"She remembered the number on the tag. She sort of has a photographic memory for details like that. Anyway, she just called to tell me she was listening to her scanner last night, off duty. She heard the call for an ambulance and county medical examiner to some railroad crossing up north in Emporium. A train had hit a Silverado with those plate numbers and the driver killed. The truck was stopped on the tracks when it was hit. They said it looked like suicide. The officer released his name over the scanner because, well... they were still trying to extract the body. His name was Tom Dresden."

"Why would he kill himself, if he was a hit man?" asked Marti. "By the way, they will do a complete tox screen with the autopsy."

"If there is anything left of him," Jayne remarked.

Both Johanna and Marti looked at her.

"Just saying," Jayne said.

"Well, that's kind of the point," said Johanna, "without anything to tie him to the Camry driver, it looks like it was self-intended. No one knows he murdered someone."

"I can look into this guy and work behind the scenes to find the name of the Camry driver. But what bothers me is this. You haven't mentioned a state highway accident report on the shooting of the Camry driver. Haven't they released the name, yet? Shouldn't you wait for that?"

"The only thing mentioned in the news was a vehicle accident on the road by the Ice Mine Cut. The driver was not identified. It doesn't mention she was shot. My friend said the vehicle was disabled, not crashed. The Camry was forced off the road."

"It certainly looks like it," said Jayne.

"So we have a dead sex trafficker, an emotionally injured child, and a hit man crushed by a train," said Marti. "Sounds like the state police are keeping it hushed for a reason."

"Investigation," asked Jayne.

"One hopes," responded Marti.

Johanna shook her head. She looked at the photo on her cell. The man was looking straight at Angelique when she photographed him. What would cause him to take his own life a few days later? Why choose a freight train instead of shooting himself?

She took a bite of her veggie burrito. He had the means, she decided, but not the will. "He was murdered!"

"Possibly, but why?" Said Marti. She pulled the bowl of street corn to her plate and took a generous helping. "I recommend the corn."

Jayne held out her hand and Marti handed the bowl to her.

"He knew too much," Jayne said.

"Possibly, but what?" Marti sampled her quesadilla. "Oh my God, this is good."

Johanna dipped some chips in the spicy salsa.

"His employers hired him to kill the trafficker," she said. "Hence, they had to kill him, too."

"And the child too, which someone probably considered an asset in a sex trafficking business," said Jayne, "but why 'off' your investment?"

"Sorry," she said to Johanna and Marti, "just saying."

"Jayne's right," responded Joanna.

"Unless the child had become a liability instead of an asset," remarked Marti.

"It stands to reason. The child knew too much," stated Jayne flatly.

"What if the child was the real target?" said Marti, thoughtfully. "He had to take out the trafficker too. Then your friend shows up and spoils the plan. His employers don't like failures, so they killed him, thereby removing the evidence."

"Then they are still after the child," said Jayne. "Loose ends, right?"

"That's one really good reason to keep her hidden. The state police don't know she exists," remarked Johanna. "So even if they hushed the shooting, they don't suspect a guy getting hit by a train in another county to have been involved."

"Knowing the victim's history helps determine why someone would have shot her. I will focus on her," said Marti.

"She's a trafficker," argued Jayne, "a perpetrator!"

"A murder victim now," said Johanna.

"But," Jayne pointed out, "the bad guys are looking for a little girl. If the hit man told his bosses what happened and he's dead so he probably did, then they were looking for her. And you have no idea who these people are. But from the sounds of it, they won't stop until they find her. By the way, what could the girl know that would get her killed?"

"We are doing our best to keep her safe. My friend drove her far away from the accident scene. There is no way the hit man would have followed her without her knowing."

"We know that for sure," said Jayne, "because he's dead and his bosses are pissed."

"Just saying," she said at Marti and Johanna's expressions.

"Quite possibly," Marti offered. She finished the last of her quesadilla and wiped her hands on a napkin. "But what if he saw enough of your friend to give a description to his bosses? What if they are looking for her?"

"Then," finished Jayne, "she should not go back to the place the child is being kept. They should all be on high alert!"

"Just saying," said Marti dryly, looking at Jayne fondly.

"I will text her. We have a secure communication link."

"What about you? Your friend brought you into this. How safe are you?" asked Marti.

"I think it's best if she and I are not seen together," responded Johanna. "Um, please, what are your rates? I want this to be all above board. I can do a secure payment on line."

Marti sighed and looked at Jayne.

The intimacy between these two women is far deeper than a new relationship, thought Johanna. It's like they have known each other for a lifetime, maybe more.

Jayne spoke first.

"A child is involved. We can't take payment for that. Consider it gratis."

"There is no way I will profit from taking down a sex ring," stated Marti. "Whatever you need from us, you have it!"

Johanna felt humbled and grateful. She never expected this response.

"There is only one thing, though," Jayne smiled. "Next time we meet, the dinner is on you!"

Johanna linked both Marti and Jayne to the secure communication app. She then texted them each a copy of Angelique's cell phone photo. They agreed to meet again when Marti had more information, this time in a more discreet location. By then, Johanna thought, *I might be able to tell them everything we have discovered.*

She returned to her room for the night. The Glen was quiet and peaceful, which was just what she needed before making the long drive back to Elk Run. She texted Scott. *"I miss snuggling up to you."*

He responded with only a heart emoji and she felt a little disappointed. She nestled deeply in the white duvet, feeling its comforting softness yet feeling very alone. She drifted into a troubled sleep surrounded by the opulently designed but emotionally barren hotel room.

A few hours later, the insistent buzzing of her cell phone awakened her. Its softly illuminated screen announced the time was 2:35 in the morning and a text from Jayne flashed by.

"We can't sleep. Are you awake too?

Well, now I am, she thought.

"What's up?" she texted back.

"We are," was Jayne's response. *"The connecting door is open. Come on over."*

Johanna swung her feet over the side of the bed and wandered through the doorway between their suites. Soft golden light spilled from the bedroom beyond the kitchenette. She stood at the entrance to the room with her long silver hair pulled into a tousled ponytail and shielded her eyes from the light.

Jayne and Marti were sitting tailor fashion on a king size bed playing cards. Jayne patted a space on the bed beside her and Johanna shuffled over and sat down on the edge of the bed. Jayne was wearing a teal blue nightgown of glimmering satin with off-the-shoulders lace straps. Marti slouched forward in her sweatpants and a crumpled Cheap Trick T-shirt that had clearly seen better days.

"We couldn't sleep, so we made a pot of green tea. Want some?"

Johanna nodded.

"Do you have any 8's," asked Marti, peering at the cards she held.

"Go fish, "Jayne responded.

"Seriously?" Johanna rubbed her head.

"Yeah, at this hour, we don't have the brains for anything more strategic."

"We try to bore ourselves back to sleep." Marti yawned. "Years of working the graveyard shift at the station make for a lifetime of sleep disorders."

"There's a cure for that," Johanna said. "Valerian tea and melatonin."

"Do you have any 5s?"

Marti threw down two cards and Jayne snatched them up.

"The only thing missing," said Marti, "is cookies."

"I know where we can get cookies," replied Johanna.

Both Marti and Jayne put down their cards and stared at her. "At this hour?"

"We can raid the bakery."

"What bakery?" asked Marti.

"The one in the mansion," Johanna replied. "We did it all the time when I worked here."

"You mean they bake those delicious cookies here on the premises?' Jayne asked.

"Twice a day," Johanna continued. "Once at noon and then they pull the second batch out of the ovens at 4:30 in the afternoon and let them cool over night before they bag them in the little cellophane packs the next morning."

"Don't they lock the place up before they leave?"

"Of course, but Security opens it up at 11PM during their rounds. They leave it open until 5AM. So we have plenty of time left to raid it."

"You're kidding," said Marti.

"No, not at all. There are a lot of guests who have trouble sleeping and wander around looking for a midnight snack. There are no vending machines in this four-star hotel, so they would corner a security guard. Security decided to leave the door of the bakery unlocked so guests can find a treat."

"How come I never knew about this?" Jayne asked.

Johanna shrugged. "I learned about it from a guard. Of course, staff would get in trouble if management knew we took cookies too, so it's a well-guarded secret."

"Where's the bakery?" asked Marti.

"It's directly under my old office wing," replied Johanna. "Do you have any dark clothes? We can't chance drawing any attention to ourselves. It would defeat the purpose. This is a clandestine operation."

"How exciting," responded Jayne with a conspiratorial grin.

Moments later, the three women walked through the hotel hallway to a side entrance clad in dark jeans and jackets. Johanna took a stone from the exquisitely landscaped shrubbery outside the entrance and placed it inside the door's lower track to keep it from fully closing.

"Follow me and walk where it's dark. Stay away from the lit sidewalk. They have security cameras pointed along all the walkways."

Johanna led the way across the grounds, walking along the oak lined property. The Gilded Age mansion was across the access road from the hotel. It was illuminated with spotlights directed at its brick facade and marble water fountain. To the right of the building was a narrow staircase concealed by a hedge of meticulously clipped hydrangea bushes. This was the employee entrance that led to the basements beneath the side towers of the mansion.

"My offices were in the rooms directly above this tower entrance," Johanna whispered.

Moments later, they opened the doors to the bakery and Johanna turned on a light. Tall racks stacked with wide trays of fresh cookies were arranged against the back wall of the room. Fragrant and familiar, the scents of cinnamon, vanilla and cardamom infused the air.

"The case of the midnight cookie heist," murmured Jayne, holding Marti's hand.

"The missing cookie caper," Marti whispered back.

"This is how we do it," said Johanna. "We each take ten cookies from several trays. You take the ginger cookies, Jayne. Marti, you nab the chocolate chips, and I will snag the macaroons. Don't steal an entire row. Snatch them from different trays. Leave lots of empty spaces on the trays or the bakers will know the same person took them all. "

There were eight large trays of each cookie variety on the racks, with about thirty cookies apiece. Hundreds of sweet confections pleasantly greeted the thieves as they pulled out the trays.

"Put five of each in both of your pockets," Johanna instructed. "If we get stopped by Security, they will never ask you to empty your pockets."

"You have clearly done this before," said Marti, sampling a chocolate chip cookie.

"Of course," said Johanna, "staff perks."

After they filled their pockets with cookies, the three women crept back to the hotel with their stolen stash of contraband confections. The moon cast its last golden rays in the darkened sky as it began its descent behind the trees. There was a murmuring of birds in the branches as they entered the side-door. Otherwise, the entire grounds and inner hallways were silent.

Back in Jayne's room, they arranged all of their cookies on three plates from the kitchenette and began to divide them up. A variety of three for each respective thief accounted for nine cookies apiece. One macaroon, one chocolate chip and one ginger cookie remained.

"You are the Queen of Thieves, Johanna," said Marti. "Take your pick!"

Johanna selected the last of the macaroons.

Jayne looked at Marti, then said," I will trade you one of my chocolate chippies for a ginger."

Marti pushed a ginger spice cookie from her stash toward the remaining two cookies. Jayne pushed a chocolate chip cookie forward. She then took the two ginger cookies and added them to her pile. Marti snagged the remaining two chocolate chips.

"Let's put on a pot of fresh tea," she said as they began to eat the looted cookies.

"It doesn't get better than this," said Jayne, munching on a ginger spice cookie.

"A purloined macaroon," said Johanna, savoring her stolen delight.

"A pinched chippie," quipped Marti.

"A filched ginger spice," finished Jayne.

They sipped tea from white porcelain cups and ate their fill of cookies. Johanna was the first to begin nodding off and retired to her suite, smiling as she closed the connecting door.

When she woke the next morning, Johanna grinned as she found cookie crumbs in her bed. She had signed up for a service at the spa salon, so she knocked on the connecting door. Jayne quickly answered and greeted Johanna with a warm hug.

"Are either of you up for an early café breakfast?"

"Marti is off for a psychic reading with Jess," Jayne said. "I have a massage."

"I am getting a manicure and a foot massage in the spa," said Johanna. "Psychic reading?"

"Marti is full of surprises."

"I am so happy for you, Jayne. You look so, well, in love."

"I am." She smiled. "So this is goodbye for now."

Johanna walked down the glass-lined walkway to the hotel spa center. She continued past the reception desk. The hair and nail salon was through the double mahogany doors at the spa entrance. She entered a room she remembered well from her years working at the hotel's heath center. It was encircled by floor to ceiling windows, filling the salon with light and a stunning view of the lushly landscaped grounds.

The attendant greeted her with a gracious smile and showed her to the pedicure room. Within moments, Johanna sat back in the warm comfort of the chair as the stylist filled the foot basin with warm water. She had booked a foot massage with coconut and sugar rub. The deeply soothing scent of lavender filled the entire space. She instantly relaxed.

The very walls of this salon held strong memories for her. The last time she was sitting in this exact chair, she and Scott had already separated. They had filed for divorce, citing irreconcilable differences. She had been attempting a self-care day in the midst of managing a difficult client load while navigating the complexities presented by the former management of the health spa hotel chain.

The previous corporation held a very high standard of excellence, from accommodations and food service to spa treatments and lifestyle consultations. The expert health and wellness team was held to an even higher standard. Staff was not only expected to stay current with their specializations, they were required to go beyond those certifications. At first, Johanna had enjoyed attending multiple yearly conferences and trainings.

The demands of being an exemplary member of an incredibly talented, skilled, and specialized team became increasingly difficult. The struggle to find balance was nearly impossible. Her marriage failed. After five years of employment, she had resigned and opened a private counseling practice in a nearby town.

By the time she and Scott divorced, Johanna could clearly see how her marriage had fallen apart. She realized now what Scott observed and tried in vain to help her understand. In the end, the spa management succeeded in exploiting her need to achieve and attain recognition for her skills. In the end, she lost what her heart held most valuable, but her mind did not fully grasp the implications of that hurt until much later.

"Have you chosen a color for your manicure yet" asked the stylist. Her voice pierced Johanna's mood of reflection.

She shook her head.

"You can make a choice from our collection in the alcove room while I prepare the station," said the stylist as she pulled the plug to empty the foot basin.

The soles of the thin plastic spa sandals made soft padded whispers on the salon floor as Johanna walked to the small room. As she entered, she saw the walls lined with glass shelves containing hundreds of colorful bottles of nail polish.

She felt inundated by the number of available choices. There was a plethora of colors and numerous finishes; creamy, glossy, frosted, and iridescent. She looked for a soft pink and was dismayed to discover about thirty different shades.

A bottle of icy pink polish caught her eye. It was on a separate shelf that was illuminated by an incandescent lamp as if it were fine jewelry. She reached for the bottle labeled "*China Smile*." But it was the nail polish bottle on the next shelf that took her breath away.

It was a bright red polish, the same color and hue as the little girl's fingers and toes had been painted. She was sure of it. She picked it up. *Ruby Tuesday*. The same name as the one registered on the kennel microchip. Johanna felt a chill move through her body. She did not believe in coincidences.

She carried both bottles of polish to the counter.

"You have wonderful taste, Ms Kincaid. That's the exclusive Chaude au Coeur line." She pronounced it *showduh' cur*. "Very expensive. Very limited. It's only found in top nail salons. Many of our male guests request certain colors for their wives. The manicure with this line of polish is rather expensive, as it includes the entire bottle. Touch up, you know. "

"Can I have my nails done in *China Smile* and buy the red polish separately?"

"Of course."

An hour later, after checking out of the hotel, Johanna walked to her car with a small salon bag swinging from her wrist. Her nails were painted the color of a dawn sunrise on the mountain. They glinted in the sunlight as she opened the car door. In the bag were two bottles of nail polish and a Chaude au Coeur brochure.

She felt sick to her stomach.

A Moon Full of Strawberries

Nadine led Willow out to the ring. Rampage was a good horse for riders learning to walk and trot. The girl was getting very steady in transitioning between the two as well as going over the trot poles. It's time for her to learn from a horse with different skills, she thought. Time to learn her leads. After many months of cross training in equitation, eventing and jumping, Nadine had discovered Willow was born for a specific purpose and it wasn't racing.

"Willow is in training for dressage," Nadine explained to the silent girl, "it's like gymnastics for horses. She is fifteen hands high. She is a chestnut like Rampage but with four white socks." She pointed to the horse's white-coated legs above the hooves.

"Stable Ticket is obviously a black thoroughbred. We have a dark bay, a dapple and a paint as well. I want you to know them by their spirits, though, not just the color of their coats. I want you to know them by their true names."

"Willow's saddle is different from hunt-seat saddles," Nadine instructed. "See, the seat is deeper and the stirrup irons are longer, the flaps are cut straight, not angled. This saddle helps the rider stay in the correct position and have closer contact with the horse. It feels different at first, maybe even uncomfortable, but you will get used to it quickly."

Nadine led Willow to the mounting block. After she settled herself into the saddle, fitting her black boots into the stirrups, the girl moved it to the side of the ring.

"Watch closely." Nadine bent her head forward slightly and Willow walked, her ears pointed forward. They made a full circle around the ring at the walk. They picked up the pace and then trotted down the center line of the ring. Willow's head curved in a muscular arc and her body moved with a combination of grace, power, and precision. At the end of the ring, Nadine turned her body slightly and Willow answered with a bend to the right, then moved diagonally across the ring to the far other side.

The horse appeared to dance across the riding ring, legs crossing over, moving both sideways and forward with each movement. The evenly spaced sound of the horse's trot beat a staccato rhythm on the earthen floor like a drum. Rider and horse moved as if they were one being. No signal from human to creature could be seen.

The pace changed to a canter as Willow's chest and forelegs came up and her whole body shifted its cadence. They seemed to be a single creature dancing diagonally across the ring as a cool breeze swept through the trees. Horse and rider were perfectly matched in movement, strength, and confidence. Nadine noticed the girl was watching them intently as they slowed down to the walk. Moments later, Nadine and Willow joined her by the gate.

"That is called a half-pass. Would you like to learn it?" The girl nodded.

Nadine dismounted and held Willow's reins while the young girl secured her riding helmet.

"First you must learn serpentines. You will learn to switch your outside leads. Like Willow did, you need to start at the beginning. Horses, especially off-the track thoroughbreds, need a job to do," explained Nadine. "Until we find out what their purpose is, they are anxious and want to run. It's all they know. While riding lessons are wonderful for you, for them it's discovering the joy of bending, reaching, and jumping."

"And so will you," Nadine said as she boosted the young rider into the saddle. She readjusted the leathers of the stirrup irons to match the girl's shorter legs. "Willow will teach you to bend and move confidently. Trust her. She has learned to trust her riders. She already knows how to do everything you ask of her."

They began in the fragile sunlight of morning. Horse and rider moved at the walk, into the trot, and the shadowed promise of a canter. A delicate liaison began to form in which the rider's timid determination began to unfold. The horse listened to the subtle pressure from the rider's legs, felt the girl's firm but gentle hands never pulling or tugging on her mouth. The horse settled into a familiar pace.

"Learn to talk to Willow using your body. But first, you must feel your own body. Feel every one of your muscles, tendons and bones with every flex, every movement," taught Nadine. "Now bend to the right and pick up the pace. Ask for the trot by squeezing your legs against her belly."

The girl squeezed her legs gently and Willow moved forward, more quickly. Her rider began to bounce in the saddle.

"Yes, that's it. Now head toward the rail. Twist your waist and hips slightly to the left, straighten, and guide her back across the ring to the other rail."

Horse and rider moved up and down the ring and back again. She turned and twisted and trotted across the ring from rail to rail. The girl hung on. She bounced and struggled to hold her balance.

"Serpentines, that's right!"

The rider began to tense. Nadine could feel the girl start to panic as she became more aware of the strength and power of the animal moving beneath her. Who knew what memories such awareness could evoke, the tall woman thought.

"They may be big, but they aren't brave," Nadine called out. "They are herd animals. If you are nervous, they will sense it. They will want to know what you are afraid of. They will start paying attention to the surroundings and less to your signals. They count on you to let them know they are safe. Find your seat. Feel your back, your hips and your shoulders. Keep your hands down. Don't let them drift up."

The constant focus on her body and its predictable movements in response to the rhythmic pace of the trot created an unexpected sensation of peace in the young girl. It was the same action over and over again as they moved up and down the ring. It was as if nothing else existed but moments of movements strung together like pearls.

Nadine watched the girl's body begin to relax and settle in. Both horse and rider were finally collected. Their wild souls were beginning to synchronize in the bending and trotting, breathing and pacing.

Her cell phone buzzed. Anita was texting her. Nadine used her phone's security app to unlock the front gate. As she watched the girl continue to ride serpentines up and down the ring, Anita joined her at the fence line.

"She is riding with more confidence," said the older woman. Nadine nodded.

"Are you sure she can handle feeling her body movements? It could be triggering bad memories."

"She is learning to trust her body and the power of the horse," responded Nadine. "She is learning to be in charge of that power."

"Good medicine," said Anita.

"Can you stay for dinner? We are having fresh strawberries with whipped cream for dessert."

"It's a full moon tonight," responded the older woman. "I will stay."

Nadine held up her arm and signaled the rider the lesson was over. The girl rode up to the fence and dismounted.

"Great job. Tomorrow you will start figure eights and learn to switch leads on your outside leg," she praised. "But for now, brush out Willow, then put her in the side corral. Can you bring the others up from the paddocks and into the barn? Leave Stable Ticket for me. Then wash up for dinner, OK?"

The girl nodded and slipped the stirrup leathers up so the irons would not bump against Willow's belly as they walked together to the barn.

Inside the farmhouse kitchen, Nadine pulled food from the refrigerator and brought in a basket of freshly picked strawberries gathered from the garden for the girl to wash and slice.

"May I take a saliva sample from you?" asked Anita.

Nadine stood quietly while the elder woman swabbed her inner cheek. The last time this happened, the doctor was taking a DNA sample to see if it was a familial match to the remains of a body uncovered in a state park. It had been.

That is how Josette found her way back to her people. She had been missing for ten years. Every morning since the day she had not returned from a shopping trip to Albany, her mother offered tobacco ties to the Creators. In the beginning, smoke prayers for her safe return wafted to the sky at dawn. Then, as the years passed, she offered smoke prayers for the return of her daughter's bones.

Nadine did not question Anita, nor did she wonder why the woman was gathering another sample. She trusted her completely.

After a light dinner of potato salad with herbs, fresh steamed green beans and cold fried chicken, the two women and the young girl sat on the front porch. As they ate strawberries, whipped cream, and shortbread, they watched a full, yellow moon rise up over the trees. All the horses were in their stalls for the night, fed and treated. The fully rounded, fragrant moon gradually illuminated the dark night sky. Bright moonlight spilled onto the farm's crescent driveway.

"They will be dancing tonight," said Anita.

"I know," responded Nadine. "I will join them again someday."

The elder woman placed her lined brown hand over the smooth, dark fingers of the younger woman. "I knew you would have some good strawberries."

Nadine thought of her beautiful daughter, who once danced in the light of another Strawberry Moon. She remembered when Josette danced beside her as a child for the first time in Grand Entry.

How proudly her daughter walked. How she looked up to the sky and saw the love of her ancestors beaming down upon her face. She remembered her daughter's true name, Pretty Dove, for the softness in her face and the delicate steps of her dance. She remembered she looked as if she was flying as she leaped in the air, and the fringes of her dance shawl spun around her.

Anita watched the young girl's face as she watched the love in Nadine's heart weave through her memories. The energy of that love radiated around her. The child bit into another strawberry and tasted the incredible sweetness of love for the very first time.

Wind Sisters

Johanna left the cabin with a wicker basket containing flowers, her four journey stones, and an old quilt. She walked along the garden pathway, weaving her way through the thyme and purslane growing around its edges. The sun was still low in the sky, the air cool in the morning hours. A mist shrouded the field beyond the wooden gate.

The grassy field lay fallow, embraced on three sides by earthen swales, harboring minerals and nutrients to support the health of future plantings. She removed her garden sandals and left them by the gate. She would walk the land in bare feet, feeling and listening for land-speak.

Angelique had taught her land has a lot to say to those who know how to listen. Eons of relationships, millions of earth turn around the sun and thousands of generations of creatures created wisdom which was gathered and held by the land itself. It was a vast and ancient library of knowledge bound into the mountain bedrock in which honor was the only currency of exchange.

It was through these connections one learned to use one's spiritual gifts; she had discovered. Intricate lessons were taught

in the various journeys to sky worlds, underworlds and
the puzzling natural environment of the middle world. The
knowledge gained through these teachings surpassed any she
had learned in graduate school.

In order to tap into this wisdom, her friend had explained,
one must learn to show respect. Many times she had referred
to her own teachers, both human and more-than-human, by
saying, "I was taught..."

Knowledge was not given freely or bestowed magically upon
seekers simply because they wanted it. One must forge careful
relationships, binding alliances with the never-born elemental
spirits. The ways of wind, rain, rivers and rocks were hidden
in plain view. Those who did not know the intricate design of
balance believed the power of storms to cleanse, flood, freeze,
or release energies as random acts of nature. It was a good thing
Johanna had some powerful allies willing to speak well of her to
these forces of nature.

As Johanna walked across the field, she shifted her pattern of
walking. "You people walk like you own the planet," Angelique
once explained. "You walk with your heels down like you own
this place. You do not. Why would power reveal itself to you
when every step you take is an assumption of ownership?
Best to keep these secrets from the ignorance of those who
would misuse them." The teaching had been punctuated by
Angelique's sparkling laughter.

She settled onto the forest floor at her sentinel place beneath the stand of oaks. She watched the woman walk across the field. She watched the muscles of the woman's legs ripple as she moved. Her own hot breath came in small snorts. She paid particular attention to the bareness of the woman's skin and her silver hair, freed from its braid, floating softly about her shoulders like a mane. Her kind hunted by watching the movements of their prey and how they behaved. She could see rings of light emanating from the woman's body. Yes, she thought, that woman is stalking some power.

Johanna walked on the dew covered grass, leading with the balls of her feet first and then setting her heals down like a soft afterthought. Just as Angelique had taught her, like walking into the Grand Entry at a Powwow, walking with respect for the lineage of Starwoman.

Listening to the bottoms of her feet wandering across the field, she felt a little tug. Here? No. There, maybe. Then she felt the nearly imperceptible hum. Yes, here.

Like dowsing with the bones of her feet rather than the crossed branches of alder, she had found the spot. Gently, she placed the basket down. Even more gently, she spread the quilt upon the ground. She then placed a circle of flowers around the quilt and the journey stones in the east, south, west and northern directions. These stones would be her guardians and they would call her back so she would not lose her way. She walked across the newly opened Eastern gate and lay down on the quilt, her spine aligned with the rock bones of the earth beneath her.

She remembered Angelique's teaching her; "a soul journey is the relinquishing of one's desire for control, a dropping of one's human robe and a donning of a different form." She breathed slowly and closed her eyes as the sky darkened above her. She felt the pulse, the drum of the Earth's heartbeat.

She exhaled, breathed, and inhaled with each perceived beat. Slowing down to a point where her own breath now seemed suspended, she slid between the spaces of those breaths and flew down a hole into the underworld.

She opened her eyes in a dimly illuminated environment of green vegetation and pale yellow sky. She felt the ground under her feet, singing and guiding her along a root-strewn path. She had been here before. She knew this path led along the ridge cliffs of the sun. It would bring her to the place where the Lady of Rainbows dwelled.

As she crossed along the top of the cliffs, she saw the gorge below crowned with waterfalls and mist through which beams of rainbow light undulated with pastel hues. She found the narrow path that descended along the wall of the cliff. She walked barefoot on the root-strewn path and descended slowly to the bottom of the gorge.

Before her was a great waterfall. A crescendo of thundering blue water cascaded into a turbulent pool below. Behind the falls, she saw the narrow opening in the rocks. Johanna walked along the pools, her body wet with mist. She walked toward the thundering falls and ducked behind a curtain of water.

A fire pit illuminated the dark cave within and she could see a figure of an old woman hunched behind the fire wearing a shawl of soft green wool. Johanna sat down before the fire and bowed her head. She felt gratitude rise within her; she felt tears slide down her face. This world was more than real; it was tangible in every way. She could feel the hardness of the ground beneath her and the moist air of the waterfall wind, the movement of air from the force of falling waters. And all of it, sentient, conscious and aware of her, as she was aware of its living presence.

The elder woman raised her head, her eyes sparkling brilliantly like starlight placed in human sockets. Johanna doubted this Being had ever been human, her form merely a formality, a compassionate response to Johanna's need for familiarity. For that, Johanna was exceedingly grateful.

The woman raised her hand and placed it in the fire. A fire that glowed fiercely yet did not burn. Johanna extended her own hand into the fire and placed it within the old woman's hand. She felt a movement as something was placed in her palm. A fringed leather medicine bag with something hard and tubular within it. She withdrew her hand and held the gift.

The words, "bring this secret into the daylight" formed in her mind. Johanna nodded. The woman's hand remained palm up in the center of the dancing fire. Reciprocity was required.

Johanna removed the citrine ring from her little finger. She placed it in the woman's open hand. It was accepted. The old woman nodded, closed her eyes and bent her head. When she raised her head again, the starlight in her eyes was gone and the fire was reduced to glowing embers. Sightless eyes stared ahead.

Johanna rose, clutching the medicine bag. She nodded respectfully and left the cave. Slowly, she retraced her steps along the pool below the falls. She walked along the narrow cliff path up along the top of the waterfalls. The clouds began to move in the sky and uncovered the face of the sun. Bright light warmed her eyelids, and she returned.

Johanna opened her eyes to find the sun had risen higher in the sky and the mist in the field had melted in the warmth of the air. She remembered how the tube in the medicine bag felt, yet her hand was empty and her citrine ring was gone. A gentle wind circled around her quilt. It touched her face and lifted her hair. Kissed by a wind sister. She was honored.

Chaude au Coeur

L ater that morning, Johanna received a secure text from Angelique requesting they meet privately. She had something to share. Johanna did as well. They agreed to meet in Cross Fork at Millie's Kettle Creek Cafe. It was a few miles down the mountain from the solar farm over a rutted washboard of a road that descended about four hundred feet over a distance of three miles. One drove slowly on this road as much for the steep elevation without guard rails as for the creatures that frequently crossed it as they moved through the dense forest.

She headed out, knowing she would arrive first. Cross Fork was a rural town along Kettle Creek in the Pennsylvania Wilds. It had been a thriving logging town over a century ago, but with the decline of logging, deforestation and a number of lumber mill fires, the town had fallen on hard times. Resilient people can carve a sustainable life even in the toughest of times. The town was the nexus of interwoven all-terrain vehicle roads throughout the Wilds.

A post office, general store, and town hall along with two food establishments and a number of cabins for rent offered hunting, fishing and other sports enthusiasts a taste of rural recreation. The businesses were thriving due to the town's collective endeavor. Millie's Kettle Creek cafe was a rustic, home-cooked food establishment with a few rooms for rent upstairs and picnic tables along the banks of the creek.

As Johanna rounded the bend before the steep decline, she saw a shadow move in the trees. As she slowed down, a bear walked out onto the road like a cautious pedestrian navigating a country road. She watched it stroll across the steep embankment and disappear into the forest on the other side. It took no notice of her.

Driving on, she rounded the last bend and crossed over the creek bridge. She parked her car in Millie's parking lot and walked over to an oak picnic table by the creek. No one else was there at this time of day. She had brought the salon bag containing her nail polish and brochure. She waited.

She heard two crows calling one another through the forest. "Cross Fork is a very quiet town," she thought, "except for the ATV weekends and the rattlesnake round-up in the summer." During the week, there was no rumbling of trucks, no sounds of industry or invasive music from passing cars. Any sound of human habitation was instantly muted, as if the trees and undergrowth gently absorbed it.

The creek was not high at the bend and she could only hear a trickle as its gentle flow moved over the rocks. The coo of a mourning dove and the answering chirps of chickadees softly pierced the stillness. Johanna heard Angelique's truck as it entered the parking lot. Waving, she met her at the entrance of Millie's.

"Hola, want to order some food? It's deliciously homemade," she called out.

They entered the small cafe.

"Coffee is great here and so are the baked goods," Johanna said, pointing to the chalkboard menu that was hung over the counter. "Just make sure you don't choose the hunter blend."

"I'll have a blueberry muffin," Angelique said to the woman leaning on the smooth oaken counter top. She was a dour faced middle-aged woman wearing a blue t-shirt, with an elk silk screened on it and the words - *stand your ground*.

"Coffee too," she added. The woman pointed to the serve-yourself buffet table with a series of three coffee canisters.

"This is all together," Johanna stated to the woman as she stepped up to order.

Angelique nodded. She stood at the buffet table and surveyed her choices. There were three choices of coffee with a plus sign to indicate strength; The Hiker+, The Fisherman++, and The Hunter+++. She selected The Fisherman's blend, pouring the pungent dark liquid into a black metal camper cup and added a splash of cream.

"Can you pour me a cup of The Hiker with extra milk?" asked Johanna as she paid for the order, adding another blueberry muffin.

"Wimp," noted Angelique, earning a stiff smile from the woman at the counter.

As they left the cafe, Angelique leaned over to Johanna and whispered, "Millie?"

The shorter woman shrugged. "No one has ever met Millie as far as I know. And no one dares ask."

They selected a picnic table by a section of the creek with a wide rock strewn bed. The creek water chirped and sang around the stones that crossed the width of the waterway. It was set away from the other tables. Johanna sipped her mildly brewed coffee as she opened a small bag and retrieved her muffin.

"There is something I have to show you," Angelique said, setting her camper cup on the table.

She held up her cell phone, which displayed a website for the Little Mountain Saluki Kennels.

"It's an exclusive show dog breeder," she explained, "run by a hotel chain owner named Anthony Tonhauer. He owns the Beau Jardin hotels in Philadelphia, New York, the Florida Keys and the Grand Bahamas. Apparently Salukis are a personal favorite of his. The breed lines of his dogs are sought after by the very wealthy. Here are some of the names in his show line: Russian Sable, Little Minx, China Smile and Indigo Star. Fast Lane and Rosa Linda are both listed as retired. And look, this one, Ruby Tuesday."

She looked up. "Why would our little deer have a show dog's microchip embedded in her shoulder?" asked Angelique.

"Did you say China Smile?" Johanna turned visibly pale.

"Yes, why?"

Johanna felt her throat tighten. She opened her salon bag and placed the bottle of red nail polish on the oak table. She withdrew the brochure.

"Every single Saluki name you just mentioned is also the name of a Chaude au Coeur polish and matching lipstick color, including Ruby Tuesday." She put the brochure on the table so Angelique could see.

She picked up the ruby red nail polish.

"This is the same color as the polish on the little girl's fingers and toes," she said, her voice barely a whisper. "And this, is the color called China Smile." She held up her newly manicured fingers.

Angelique read the brochure. The exclusivity of the cosmetic line, the ability to order on-line and the availability for purchase along with colors that were no longer available matched perfectly with the breed dogs on-line, which were either also available or retired.

The two women looked at each other. Neither woman moved.

"This is no coincidence," said Johanna, "I wonder who owns the Chaude au Coeur line. It says the company is based in Florida. How on earth can we move forward on this?"

"I have no idea but I will find out," said Angelique. "We have circumstantial connections between a dog kennel, a cosmetic line, and a sex trafficking ring. The same person who owns an exclusive hotel chain that is known to be a frequent choice of celebrities and other high-profile customers may run all of them. The hotel chain is so exclusive, neither you nor I could afford a single night's stay."

Angelique put the brochure down on the table. She looked out over the creek. The sounds of the water and the call of birds spoke of balance and harmony, none of which either woman could feel in their bones that moment. The disturbance was visceral, the dread tangible.

After a few moments of silence, Johanna looked up. "I took a journey this morning in the field. I saw the Lady of Rainbows. She gave me a gift. A medicine bag with a hard, tube-shaped object in it. She told me to bring its secret out into the daylight."

Angelique looked away momentarily, then returned her gaze toward Johanna. "You have been honored. The Lady of Rainbows knows the level of your skills. She also respects your willingness to stand in the shadows of Spirit. We all know even master shamans are still students in the eyes of their teachers. It's all too easy for human egos to believe they themselves are orchestrating this power."

She continued, "Spirit brought me to the Ice Mine Cut at precisely the moment in which my presence spared a child's life. It does not surprise me in the least that Spirit is intervening in other ways."

"There is something more," offered Johanna. "It seems the man you saw at the Cut was murdered a few days ago. He was in his truck when it was hit by a freight train."

That was a surprise that rocked Angelique's usual calm composure. Johanna told her about the call from her daughter and the conversation with Marti and Jayne at The Glen.

"Marti is digging into the dead woman's identity and learning more about the hit man, Tom Dresden. She will meet with me when she has any information."

"I want to be at that meeting," said Angelique. "This is a very complex situation. We need to understand why someone would name cosmetics after show dogs. We need to understand what's happening here and how we can keep this child safe."

"Don't you think it's obvious?" said Johanna carefully. "Men order a 'Saluki' for their personal use. The girl's name is also a dog's name. She is wearing a signature color lipstick and matching nail polish by the same name. Look here," she pointed to the brochure. "The color 'Fast Lane' is no longer available in the brochure and listed on the kennel website as 'retired.'"

"Maybe," she continued, "this is how they order and pay for a trafficked girl. The on-line availability of the dog correlates with an available cosmetic. Oh, there is something else."

"The salon manager at The Glen, a spa hotel for the same clientele as the exclusive hotel you mentioned, told me that male guests often purchase Chaude au Coeur products. They order a particular shade of nail color for their wives. Some of those men are wealthy enough to afford more than a few nights at Beau Jardin."

Angelique's eyes grew sharper. "Are you implying they like to see the nail and lipstick color worn by one of the trafficked girls on their own wives?"

"Yes, that's the level of depravity we are dealing with here."

"That is particularly disturbing. These people lost their humanity a long time ago."

"How does Spirit think we can stop this?"

"The Creators are not within our capacity to understand," Angelique said softly. "They are not linear. They will offer us direction as we need it. They have called us together for the very gifts they have given us. They will use us however they need in order to restore balance. Their way."

Angelique leaned over the table and placed her butterfly tattooed hand on Johanna's pale wrist. They looked into one another's eyes.

"What is your next step, Sister? That is the question here. The Lady has clearly called you into action."

She Claims her Voice

J uly was a hot month. There would be no training on this lazy Sunday morning, Nadine thought as she walked down to the paddocks. She was thinking a picnic ride and dip in the ponds off Sugarcamp Road sounded good. The girl could ride Rampage who needed some trail experience. She would ride Merlin, who had just been put up for sale.

She saw the girl leaning against the fence surrounding Stable Ticket's paddock. From the far side, the black thoroughbred charged the gate. The girl stood rooted to the spot as the horse ran at her with his ears pinned back. She sang to him softly and the horse suddenly pulled up, sliding on his haunches like a barrel racing quarter horse. His ears came forward; he lowered his head and walked toward her. He nudged her hand, and she laughed.

A moment passed, then the girl spoke. "You are beautiful," she said, stroking the horse's face. He nickered.

Nadine stood perfectly still and then said, "you, too, are beautiful."

The girl spun around. Nadine noticed for the first time her curly jet black hair perfectly matched the color of the racehorse's shiny black coat.

"Would you like to go on a trail ride today?"

The girl nodded.

Nadine walked over to the paddock gate. "Let me show you something," she said as she held Stable Ticket's halter. "You know these horses are racers that have outlived their racing lives. We retrain them for a second life here at the stable."

The girl nodded.

"Sometimes it's hard for them to forget their other lives because running is all they have ever known. But they are beautiful, wild creatures and their kind have survived for thousands of years. Our job is to remind them of that so they can have the life the Creators wanted for them, not what humans planned."

"Here, see this?" Nadine held the horse's mouth with one hand and lifted his lip with the other. A number was tattooed on his upper lip.

"This is how they identify a certain race horse that belongs to an owner," she continued. "They are marked for life. But here at this barn, Spirit gives them a new life and their one true name."

"Can people do that?"

"Yes, they can. You are finding the true life the Creators wanted you to have," Nadine responded. "Let's get these horses fed and turned out. After stall cleaning, we can plan a picnic, OK?"

The girl nodded, "OK."

Nadine decided to text the others later and let them know about the new development. Their little deer was talking. They would have to go slowly. Like learning to walk over trot poles or jump a rail, time and trust was everything.

A few hours later, they saddled up Rampage and Merlin. Each rider had a backpack containing sandwiches, snacks, treats, and towels. They rode to the back of the barn and headed down a well-marked trail to the ponds.

The forest was cool, shaded by trees of deep green with thick underbrush at their trunks. The air danced with the sweet scent of pine. A blue sky was laced with dark shadowed impressions of tall branches over head. Squirrels dashed out of their way and birds called to one another as they slowly rode by.

"Be attentive. Rampage is not used to trail rides yet. His sense of herd and safety comes from the track and stables. You are his herd now. He will look to you like a lead mare."

The girl sat strongly in the saddle, legs draped around the racehorse's belly, her hands firmly on the reins. She had been riding daily for the past three months and her training was beginning to be evident. "Let your body be firm but relaxed. Firm because you are in charge, relaxed because you need to let him know there is nothing to fear here in the forest," Nadine instructed.

"It's like an enchanted forest, isn't it?"

"How so?"

"Everything is so green and alive, everything smells earthy and fresh. It's like something magic can happen."

"Wait till you see the ponds."

"Can we swim?"

"Yes, and so can the horses."

They rode on, bearing to the left as the trail forked. Nadine took a chance. Rampage was ahead of Merlin, so she could not see the girl's face.

"What is your name?" she asked carefully.

"They called me Ruby," her voice became childlike. "I think I had another name, but I don't remember it."

"May I call you 'Granddaughter,' asked Nadine. "For my people, it's a name of respect."

Momentarily, there was only silence.

"Is that my one true name?"

"That will come later."

"Will I have to go back to the kennels?" Her body stiffened.

"You can stay here with me, as long as you want, child. You are safe here."

They rode on silently. A tear burned the corner of Nadine's eyelid. Her heart was heavy and a deep sadness descended through her body. It held a depth of pain she had not felt since learning of Josette's death.

They came to a clearing and an expanse of water after rounding a bend with a slight rise of the forest floor. Several ponds came together, here, weaving nets of water, teaming with fish and water birds.

They slipped off the horses and led them to the edge of the pond. They wore bathing suits under their shirts and jeans. Nadine unsaddled the horses and made a small camp in the clearing. The girl gave a few treats to the horses.

"Swim first, picnic after," said Nadine. "We go bareback and nudge them into the pond." The tall Indian woman boosted the girl onto Rampage's bare back, then used a flat rock to mount Merlin. They walked the horses into the pond. It was a hot day made cooler by the wet, refreshing chill of the water.

They heard a whinny from the hill as a pony and rider came into view. A teenage boy waved at them. Nadine returned the wave. This time when the girl stiffened, Rampage's head came up and Nadine could feel her fear.

"It is Sam Red Deer's son," Nadine said. "He is a good person. It's OK."

The girl looked at the boy warily. He was about sixteen years old and as tall as a man to her.

"Hey, hey, Fox," Nadine called out.

They walked the horses back onto the beach. Nadine slipped off Merlin and handed the reins to the girl. Fox dismounted.

"My granddaughter," Nadine indicated, and the boy nodded.

"I heard Merlin was ready to be sold."

"Yes. Are you interested?"

He nodded.

"Come by the farm and ride him. I haven't listed him yet. We can talk price if he is right for you."

"I would like that."

Fox stood by Merlin and looked at his confirmation. The horse had strong lines, was heavily muscled, and his legs were healthy. Many ex racehorses had bad legs from being run constantly.

"He is good with Western as well as English saddle," she said. "He could be pleasure as well as dressage, but he loves to jump."

"I have been wanting a jumper," Fox said with a smile.

"We will put up some rails when you come by. You can see how he moves."

Fox mounted his pony and smiled at Ruby, who quickly looked away from him. He rode off over the hill.

Moments later, the horses' reins tied to a tree, Nadine and the girl sat on beach towels eating their sandwiches.

"Was it hard for you?" Nadine asked, her voice as soft as a horse's nicker.

"Yes. Every day, I thought I was going to die. Sometimes, I wanted to because then it would all be over."

"Do you remember much?"

She shook her head and replied, "it's mostly foggy but I still see things, men's faces, in my head. Laney said they drug us so we won't remember much."

"Laney?"

"She was one of the older girls. My mother gave me to her." She shivered, and Nadine placed her sweater around the girl's shoulders.

"Sometimes I thought I had died. Everything was quiet. It was dark, but nothing hurt. But then the sun would rise and pink light would fill my kennel cage and that's how I knew it was a new day. That's how I knew I was still alive."

Nadine wanted to reach out, to hug, hold, console, and protect her. But she also knew from working with injured animals, the girl's body would react violently to touch. Healing would come from knowing her body was not being harmed. Nadine touched the young girl with her voice instead.

"You are safe with me, here on the farm. I will make sure no one hurts you. That is what a grandmother does. We keep the children safe."

A short while later, they rode back to the barn and unsaddled the horses. Nadine's cell phone buzzed, and she pressed the gate button on the security panel. Within a few minutes, Anita drove into the yard.

"I just came by to see if I could get one of Josette's old hair brushes."

Nadine nodded. She went into the farmhouse.

"You're one of the aunties, "said the child.

"Yes," answered Anita, laughing. "The medicine auntie."

Anita watched the girl groom the horses and then lead them into their stalls. She saw her lean against the Stable Ticket's stall door as the racehorse stamped the floor. The girl did not flinch or step back.

Anita could see things much the same way that Johanna did, but with an intensity that was nearly unbearable. She not only saw what happened to injured people, she saw things as if the experience was actually happening to herself. It had begun with an accident victim on the reservation many years ago when she was a young girl. She saw the accident through the eyes of the person who was mangled in the car wreck.

A Medicine Person explained to her this gift was very difficult. She would not be able to prevent herself from seeing things, but she could learn to help the victims. She studied hard and eventually went to college. She became a medical doctor to help heal the injuries she saw in her visions.

She knew how to help the young girl who stood before her now. She saw exactly what she had encountered. She saw the faces of the men who had harmed her. She could identify one in particular, but her vision in itself proved nothing. She could, however, help this child recover by other means.

Anita recalled her vision of the moment of Josette's death. She saw the face of the white man who raped and murdered her. These were things she could not bear to tell Nadine. But this young girl could be saved and Anita knew exactly what she needed to do. True justice did not merely mean the enforcement of a law; it also meant safety from further harm.

Nadine returned with her daughter's hairbrush in a plastic bag and handed it to Anita.

"I'll return it later," the doctor promised.

Neptune's Diner

J ohanna drove the Subaru as Angelique sat 'shotgun' in the passenger seat beside her. It was a long drive to meet Marti and Jayne at the halfway mark between the Pennsylvania Wilds and Philadelphia. Johanna had received a secure text from Jayne the day before suggesting they meet at a diner in Newburgh, NY, just off the New York Thruway. They had some new information to share.

Marti had booked a private back porch meeting room at the Neptune Diner. The restaurant was on a back road near an airport. If Angelique and Johanna were being followed, it would be easy to notice and reschedule their meeting for another time and place.

"Tell me again," asked Angelique, "how you know them?"

"I met Jayne at The Glen when I worked in integrative medicine. She was a guest who booked my energy healing and hypnotherapy services. Over the years, we became friends. When I opened my private practice in the Berkshires, she designed my office space. She is an architect and Feng Shui practitioner."

Angelique nodded her head as she watched the curving road that wound through the mountains. Two pairs of eyes were better than one when dodging leaping deer and slow-moving elk.

"Marti?"

"She is Jayne's partner, as in love. She is an ex-Philly police officer who took over running her uncle's detective agency. Funny as hell," said Johanna, "she doesn't miss a thing."

"I am happy about her confidentiality as a detective, less so about the ex law enforcement background. We can tell her a lot, but we still can't disclose the child's location."

"Agreed. When I told them you wanted to meet them, I said you were involved in the child's rescue. I did not identify you by your full name or mention you were the witness at the Ice Mine Cut."

A cell phone buzzed and Angelique looked down at the console where Johanna's cell phone rested, then her own phone buzzed. Two text messages were incoming. Angelique reached for her phone.

"It is Anita," she said, scrolling through the group messages. "She says the Jane Doe tox screen came back with Rohypnol metabolites. That and an STD, but she doesn't specify."

"How long since she was roofied?" asked Johanna.

"Let me ask," Angelique said as she texted Anita. "So that's why she was so limp in the car and non-responsive to the shooting. I thought she was in shock. But she was actually coming down from paralysis. She could speak until she realized she could be killed for what she knew!"

Weekend traffic on the New York Thruway was always a challenge as it converged onto three major highways leading to New York City, Philadelphia, and Newark. Jayne fancied herself a frustrated race car driver. Growing up, she rode motorcycles and drove fast cars. Marti had survived many a high-speed chase in Philly, but doubted she would survive Jayne's weaving through the slower traffic at break neck speed in a vintage Shelby Cobra Mustang. She gripped the leather armrests as if she was being launched from a rocket.

"You just like to be in control," Jayne quipped fearlessly.

"What's wrong with that?"

"Nothing at all," responded Jayne. "In certain situations, it's quite pleasurable!" Marti blushed.

"Anita says she was given Rohypnol within 24 to 36 hours of the blood draw," stated Angelique, reading an incoming text.

Johanna nodded as she slowed down to take the exit onto Route 84 toward Scranton. They were nearly half way to the meeting place.

"It may be a small blessing she was given Rohypnol," offered Angelique softly. "Her memory of the more traumatic parts of what she has endured may be spotty and she may not have felt any pain."

Johanna sped onto the highway, looking in her driver side mirror. "Or sporadic, disjointed segments of horror interspersed with physical shock," she said bluntly. "The body records everything, even if the mind is relatively unconscious. Now that she has regained her voice, we may learn more."

"Nadine is taking it slow. She knows the story will come out in its own time, if at all. Besides the girl's location, is there anything else you think we need to leave out?"

"I think we need to put everything else we know on the table. But I don't think we should mention the girl is talking."

"I agree," said Angelique. "I am fine letting them know I am the one that took the picture at the Cut and rescued her."

"Then we will have an ex-cop who will know the identity of a person who is a primary witness to a crime and who also knows the location of a victim."

Angelique sighed and looked out the passenger car window. They drove silently for about thirty miles before she spoke again.

"Something has to give here," she said. "My heart says I need to believe that Spirit has called together a band of warriors who must trust one another implicitly. If we are to succeed, it will not only be to rescue our little deer but to put an end to this ring of predators and free more children from this abuse."

"We can count on Nadine and Anita to keep her safe," said Johanna. "We need to do whatever it takes to stop these jackals, however high it goes, however far their privileged circle extends."

Angelique reached over and clasped Johanna's free hand in a tight grasp. "No Cinderellas here," she said.

***

The New York Thruway was not for pussies. The amount of travel resulted in traffic jams, accidents and frayed nerves. Jayne made up for lost time by gunning the Mustang. Marti's nerves frayed a little more.

"I am really happy you learned so much about the drivers. I hope it helps solve the case!"

"This case is a long way from being solved," responded Marti. "I'm hoping any new information Johanna has shows us what direction to take. Right now, only law enforcement can stop the sex traffic ring and that's a really big 'if.'" Without identifying the child, there is really nothing to go on."

They were half an hour out of Newburgh when Marti texted Johanna their estimated time of arrival was sooner than expected. "We will go on in and order a buffet lunch," she wrote.

Nearly a half hour later Angelique pointed out the landmark indigo blue sign and silver trident of the Neptune Diner and Johanna pulled into the parking lot. She parked the Subaru a short distance away from Jayne's distinctive black Mustang convertible with its vibrant pink racing stripe. Johanna remembered Jayne's passion and support for cancer survivors and how she insisted on a custom paint job. No simple pink ribbon on a bumper for her.

The Neptune Diner was a vintage dinner train car with distinctively rounded metal walls. The two women entered the restaurant through a small portico flanked by planters filled with bright flowers of patriotic hues. They were greeted by a cacophony of cooking smells and the murmuring of the diner's patrons.

The hostess directed them to a door at the end of the dinner car, which opened onto a small porch. The meeting room was spacious with a buffet table, hot coffee urn, teapot and 'help-yourself' stacks of dishes and cups. Screened windows with white eyelet curtains overlooked a well-maintained flower garden. It was an intimate room furnished with small round tables laid with vintage 1950's pink rose painted cotton tablecloths.

Jayne and Marti stood up as they entered. "The coffee is quite good here," announced Marti. "Organic, free trade. They are bringing us a sandwich tray."

"Angelique, this is Jayne Cullen and Marti O'Neil. Jayne, Marti, this is Angelique, my friend and mentor," said Johanna.

"Boudreau, Angelique Boudreau. I am the person who took the picture at the Ice Mine Cut."

Johanna breathed deeply.

"How incredibly brave of you," said Jayne, "not only to have thought to snap a picture but to actually go right up to the car!"

Angelique nodded, "some things are automatic. I am afraid getting into trouble is second nature to me. But in this case it was a child in trouble."

"The right person at the right time," Marti offered. "But I don't believe in coincidences."

The wait staff briskly entered with trays carrying a selection of sandwiches and snacks of fruit and cheese. As the door closed, Marti said, "I know the owners. They are discreet and won't disturb us."

As they sat down, Johanna pulled out her wallet, "it's my turn. Maybe I should settle the bill before we start?"

"Oh I already paid," said Jayne.

"Venmo me and I will reimburse you," said Johanna.

"That works!"

A few moments later the four women were seated at a table with cups of steaming coffee and sandwiches as they organized their notes.

"The tomato, mozzarella and basil sandwich is delicious," Johanna exclaimed.

Marti nodded as she put two mini subs on her plate. Jayne selected a roast beef and caramelized onion roll up while Angelique filled a bowl with chili and tortilla chips.

"This reminds me of my days on the force when we were pulling all nighters on tough cases. The way to focus on important details is to fill your stomach with food, calms you down. Nothing quite like a bunch of keyed up, tense cops to miss something important," Marti sighed. "Although, we never ate so well, it was always pizza or Mexican take-out."

"I was thinking we should present our information in the order we became involved. That gives as much chronological basis as possible," said Johanna. "That also means Angelique goes first."

Jayne placed a small notebook on the table and took a pen from her shoulder bag. She looked up intently as Angelique began to speak, starting her story after she rescued the child from the car.

"When I brought the little girl, named Jane Doe for our purposes, to a safe place, I arranged for a doctor to do a medical exam. We had no idea what she had experienced. She was withdrawn and only spoke briefly when I took her from the scene. Afterward, she completely stopped talking and I assumed it was shock. During the course of the exam, the doctor who was doing a rape kit, noted a small, hard bump under her skin by the back of her shoulder. It was an object embedded in her skin." Angelique was silent for a moment, letting this revelation sink in.

"The doctor excised it and found it to be a small microchip, the kind vets insert into animals," she continued. "We had it scanned by a vet we know. It was registered to a dog kennel in Pennsylvania," she continued.

'The Little Mountain Saluki Kennel is owned by Anthony Tonhauer. He also owns an exclusive hotel chain called the Beau Jardin which is booked by extremely wealthy patrons, celebrities and politicians from around the world."

"The address of the dog kennels is 102 Sandy Springs Road, Eastville, Pennsylvania. The microchip included the name: "Ruby Tuesday" which is a show dog's name listed in their on-line brochure of dogs available for mating." Angelique placed a printout of the kennel's online brochure on the table.

Jayne gasped and dropped her pen on the floor. "Is she okay? That poor child!"

"Yes," said Angelique, "she is recovering and in good hands. There was evidence of recent rape and unfortunately ongoing sexual abuse. The doctor texted me on our way here, to say the tox screen had come back with evidence of Rohypnol that had likely been administered within 24 - 36 hours of her blood draw. It was the effects of that date rape drug that I was observing, not shock as I thought."

" Rohypnol? It sounds vaguely familiar,"said Jayne.

"It's a surgical anesthetic used by rapists to drug their victims," offered Marti, "illegal, not even medical doctors can use it in this country. It renders a person nearly paralyzed within minutes and is commonly slipped into a drink at a bar or party. Minutes later, the rapist escorts their intended victim out as they rapidly become incapacitated. We called it being roofied."

Marti then looked down at her cell phone intently, her face a mixture of tight emotions.

"So she couldn't fight back," stated Jayne as she picked up her pen and sighed.

"Hardly," responded Angelique. She looked at Johanna.

"There's more," said Johanna, picking up the story. She opened the salon bag from The Glen and placed the cosmetic brochure on the table along with the bottle of red nail polish.

Jayne reached over and picked up the nail color. "Chaude au Coeur, this is expensive stuff!"

"Exclusive, too," responded Johanna. " I attended the medical exam and not only was the name of this nail color the same as the show dog on the microchip, the little girl had recently received a professional manicure and pedicure with this very same color."

Jayne turned over the bottle and said, "Oh my God, Ruby Tuesday!" She handed it to Marti who was looking more and more grim by the moment.

"Every nail and lipstick color in this brochure matches a show dog name on the kennel website," finished Johanna.

"I discovered the Chaude au Coeur line is owned by a company called the Tonhauer Investment Group," said Angelique.

"Can I see the salon brochure," asked Marti. "What does 'not available' mean? Here? Fast Lane?"

"We think it means a girl they retired. Look, that Saluki is not available on the website either." Johanna pointed to the name of the show dog, Fast Lane, which corresponded to the nail polish and lipstick color of the same name.

"What happens to a retired girl," asked Marti. "Do they sell her off?"

"Who knows what people like this would do," said Jayne as Marti rapidly typed into a search engine on her cellphone.

"Now the story becomes a little strange," began Johanna. "As you know, Jayne, I not only do energy healing I have been studying shamanic journeying for a long time." She looked over at Angelique who chose that moment to walk over to the buffet table.

"I took a journey a few days ago to see how I could help this child and others who were being used as sex toys. I visited the Lady of Rainbows," Johanna said.

Jayne leaned forward, intently focused. The gentlest of smiles appeared and her face radiated a beauty that was illuminated from within. Marti leaned back and crossed her arms over her chest. Her face was expressionless.

"I know this may sound weird, Marti."

"Not at all," Marti responded. "You can't imagine how normal it is to me. Both Jayne and I use spiritual means to expand our investigations. Linear logic bumps into so many obstacles whereas; non-linear thinking can provide far more possibilities. I find your methods fascinating."

"When I journeyed to the waterfalls and met with the Lady, she placed a small rawhide medicine bag in my hand. I could feel a cylindrical object inside the bag. I couldn't tell what it was. She told me it was a secret that I needed to bring into the light of day. I'm afraid that's all."

"That's very cryptic," said Jayne.

"It's how Spirit communicates in the Shamanic worlds," Angelique said softly. She returned to the table with a bowl of fruit and cheese to share with the group.

"What do you make of it," asked Marti.

"It seems important but I have no idea how it fits in," answered Johanna. "Maybe what you have to tell us will help us understand The Lady's meaning."

As Marti reached for her notes, Jayne softly placed a hand on her arm. Marti looked impatient, yet hesitated.

"Let's find out," Jayne reached into her shoulder bag. She withdrew a velvet pouch which contained an amethyst pendulum on a single silver chain. She positioned it over her left palm using her right hand. "Let's ask the dowser."

The pendulum stood still over the center of her palm as Jayne asked, "is the cylindrical object important to this investigation?"

The amethyst began to swing from side to side, slowly at first, then a quicker, wider arc.

"I'll take that as a yes," declared Marti.

Angelique smiled and nodded as if this was no surprise to her.

"Could I ask a question, Angelique," asked Jayne.

"Yes, of course."

"Are only female dogs listed on that kennel brochure?"

"I think so." Angelique gave the brochure to Jayne.

"Hmm," she looked at it carefully. "No studs, no sires. What hubris! It's like they don't even care about looking legitimate. They claim to be a show dog breeding kennel and they only have bitches."

Johanna flinched at the word.

"Bitches!" Angelique's composure melted.

"That's right," responded Jayne. "Disgusting."

"That might not be their only error," offered Marti. "Criminals tend to make them. It's how we uncover their tracks."

"What made you think to ask that, Jayne?" Johanna looked at the Chaude au Coeur brochure intently as if it bore even more secrets.

"I just love the way her mind works," Marti answered. "She sees pieces of puzzles no one else even knows are there."

"It's my architectural mind. Parts have to fit together. I see the gaps."

"Maybe my information will fill some of those gaps," said Marti, as she placed an enlarged print photo of the two vehicles at the Ice Mine Cut on the center of the table.

"I am starting with the white, Chevy Silverado, PA tags TZE2310. The truck is registered to Thomas Dresden of Philadelphia, whom we presume to be the man in the photo. Dresden, according to a local Emporium newspaper, was killed when a train hit his pickup truck earlier this week. The accident is currently under investigation by the Pennsylvania State Police."

"Dresden was employed by The Guardian Security agency," she continued. "They supply bodyguards for celebrities, corporate executives and anyone else wealthy enough to pay their exorbitant fees. The security agency issued a statement a few days ago stating the loss of their employee was devastating and they have no idea why he might have taken his own life."

Johanna drew in her breath.

"Yeah," continued Marti, "they were quick to make that point. He is registered to own and carry firearms in Pennsylvania, Utah, and Arizona which means he can legally travel with firearms just about anywhere with those permits."

"The Toyota Camry is registered to Elaine Webster of 102 Sandy Springs Road, Eastville, Pennsylvania. She has an arrest record for indecent exposure, prostitution, procurement and theft. She never gets convicted because the charges are continually dropped. She never even makes it into a court."

"Friends in high places?" Jayne looked up from her notes.

"Most likely," responded Angelique.

"Can I see that kennel listing?"

Jayne handed the website printout to Marti who scanned it with a practiced eye.

"Here it is," she said, "the address of the kennel is the same address as Elaine Webster's. The vehicle is not registered to the kennel, however."

"So Elaine Webster either lives at the kennel or she is an employee there," remarked Jayne.

"Possibly, but look at the tag on the Camry. 5ALUKI." Marti pointed to the photo on the table.

Angelique shook her head, "the 5 looks like an S, which would spell Saluki."

"What does this mean? I am having trouble putting it all together." Johanna sighed. "Everything we know are just pieces of a dark puzzle."

"What if I tell you the Tonhauer Investment Group and the Beau Jardin Hotel chain are big customers of the Guardian Security firm?" Marti sat back and took a sip of coffee. "I found that online at the agency's website, just now."

"I would say their bodyguards do double time as hit men," responded Angelique. She picked up the photo again and looked it intently.

"But why kill the trafficker if she is an employee of the very people who hired the bodyguard," asked Johanna.

"Either he was hired out by a rival client or Elaine Webster was collateral damage and possibly the target was the child all along," offered Marti.

"Why kill a child?" Johanna pushed her plate back as if she could not stomach another bite. "What could she possibly know that would warrant shooting her in broad daylight on a main road?"

Jayne leaned over and touched Johanna's wrist gently. "She must know her abusers. The identities of the men who paid for her."

Marti was watching Angelique carefully. As a seasoned investigator she had questioned fragile witnesses many times. In her experience they had seen far more than their traumatized minds initially remembered.

She noticed the slight tremor in Angelique's slender fingers as she covered one hand with the other as if the blue butterfly tattooed on it could subdue the shaking.

"Angelique, would you mind, if I asked you a few questions?"

Angelique looked up and for the first time since meeting her, Marti saw apprehension rather than confidence in her eyes.

"Tell me, from the beginning, slowly, what happened that day. Please close your eyes and go back a few hours before you drove by the Ice Mine Cut." Marti's voice was soft, gentle, and almost intimate. Jayne looked at Marti knowing they were seeing a side of her that most people would never get to know. Marti had a mind that balanced reason and logic with laser-like threads of intuition.

Angelique sat back, closed her eyes and held her hands together tightly in her lap. She began.

"It was the night before the new moon. Several people from the tribal council were meeting for a ceremony so I was up in the hills for the night. We camp out under the stars while one of us, the fire-keeper, waits for the stars to be in the right position, before dawn. We gathered and did a ceremony before the sun rose. Then we broke camp and left to go back to our homes."

She sighed but her shoulders remained tense. Johanna wanted to reach out and touch her friend's arm in support, but did not.

Angelique continued, "I was driving down the road that runs along the Hyner River as the sun started to rise. The sky was lightening up and stars were disappearing as I came down through the hills. Then I came to the tight curve by the Ice Mine Cut. I slowed down because even though I hadn't seen a single car since I left the ceremony, people coming from the other direction tend to cut that corner into the oncoming lane. It is a very tight curve."

"So you sensed you needed to slow down," asked Jayne.

Angelique nodded. Marti held up her hand, looked at Jayne and made a gesture indicating she should not ask any more questions. Jayne nodded.

"As I came around the curve, I saw the white pickup truck half in the road, half off," she paused thoughtfully. "I saw the Camry pulled off by the gated entrance to the Ice Mine. I thought at first, there's been an accident. I pulled over to help."

Angelique's voice changed. Her speech slowed down and her body became very relaxed. "I remember I picked up my phone to call 911 for road assistance and that's when I see the man. He is leaning into the driver side door of the Camry. He stands back and ... oh, oh, I see the flash. The gun went off. It is loud, like a cannon!"

No one said a word, no one moved. Soft tears rolled down Angelique's cheeks. She made no effort to stop them.

"I am holding my cell phone up," she continued slowly, "and then he aims at something in the back seat, he turns and sees me. I snap the picture when he holsters the gun. He gets in his truck and drives away.'

"I saw him murder that woman." Angelique's head bowed down. "I did not know I saw it." She began to cry.

Marti reached over and touched the blue, butterfly hand that lay quivering in the native woman's lap. "And then, what happens? What do you do," she asked softly.

"I drove up behind the Camry, got out. I have to see. I need to know what is in that car. The driver side door is still open. I look in; the driver was thrown back against the passenger side seat by the force of the gunshot. There is blood everywhere, her face is gone!"

Marti stroked the butterfly hand gently. "Go on, slowly, what else do you see?"

"There is a cosmetic case on the floor of the passenger side, makeup is all over the place. It looks like it exploded. Something weird. Her fingernails are painted kind of iridescent purple, garish with all the blood. She is holding something in the palm of her hand ..... oh!"

Angelique drew a slow breath, calming herself. "Her hand unfolded and a silver tube fell onto the floor into the rest of the makeup. I looked into the back seat and there was a child spattered with blood. She was just sitting there, still like a statue."

Jayne took Marti's cell phone. Marti gently urged Angelique to continue.

"I opened the back door and gathered the little girl in my arms. All I could think was to get out of there before he came back to kill us both. I carried her to my truck and drove away, back the way I came."

Jayne found the picture she was looking for at the Chaude au Coeur website. She nodded to Marti.

"I asked the girl if it was her mother in the car. She said, no, her mother had sold her to that woman. She called her a name, Laney. Yes, that's the name."

"Elaine Webster," responded Marti, turning to Jayne.

"Angelique," Jayne's voice was nearly a whisper. "Is this what that tube looked like?"

She held up an image on Marti's phone.

Angelique opened her eyes and stared at the cell phone. She nodded.

"That's a Chaude au Coeur lipstick tube. They're all gun metal silver and rounded at the top like little bullets," stated Jayne.

"So the cylindrical object the Lady put in my hand isn't only important to this investigation, it's crucial," Johanna said as she poured a cup of hot sweetened tea and gave it to Angelique.

"I would say so," stated Marti.

"I think we should ask the cards," said Jayne decisively.

Marti pulled a deck of well-used tarot cards from the inside pocket of her corduroy jacket. She handed them to Angelique. "Will you shuffle these?"

"Now," Marti said, reaching for a piece of cheese."Sift through the deck and select three cards, place them face down on the table."

"Do we need to ask a question," asked Johanna.

"We already have," Marti replied.

Angelique slowly shuffled and selected three cards from the deck and placed them on the table.

"We know the silver lipstick tube is important, we are about to learn why." Marti turned the first card over.

"Ah, the Devil, upright. There is a lot of power involved in this operation. It involves seduction or obsession with material pleasures. It also means living in fear or bondage."

Johanna winced and Angelique laid her hand on top of her thigh.

Marti turned over the second tarot card.

"The seven of stones," she said. "This is a business with a lot of financial backing, fraudulent operations, deceit, and dirty money."

"Well, tell us what we don't know," Jayne said sarcastically.

Marti turned over the third tarot card and drew her breath in sharply. "White Buffalo Calf Woman - reversed."

Angelique looked puzzled.

"She is the leader of my deck, the guide for my readings," responded Marti. "She creates the sacred undercurrent and purpose of the guidance the cards reveal to me."

"She is upside down," said Johanna, "does that mean our efforts will fail?"

"No," said Marti. "It means the force we are operating against isn't just criminal behavior, it's inhuman debauchery itself. Innocence is sacred. They have turned innocence into depravity. She stands for all things sacred. She is standing by our mission, by 'turning her wisdom over' to us."

"What on earth is in that lipstick tube?" said Angelique.

"We don't know, but I think it's the key to everything," said Marti. "It's time to bring in the big guns. This is bigger than all of us. I think I have an idea."

Marti laid out the bare bones of her plan.

An hour later, they gathered their notes, set their used dishes on the buffet table and prepared to leave. Jayne and Johanna took a walk in the flower garden, arms around each other's waists and heads bowed together conspiratorially.

Marti slipped into her corduroy jacket and walked over to Angelique, taking the tall, darker skinned woman's hands into her own. Dark brown eyes shining in a face the color of cream looked deeply into pools of dark, sparkling eyes held within a face fashioned by a lineage of ancestors millions of years old. Angelique's people traced their heritage back to the stars.

"I am sorry to have taken you back to that place in your mind," began Marti, sincerely. "I needed to know what you knew but couldn't think about. I'm sorry if I made you feel uncomfortable."

Angelique smiled. "It is alright. Any discomfort I felt is small in comparison with what our little deer has endured."

"Little deer?"

"Yes, that is our name for the girl, a term of affection."

The two women looked at each other, a relationship of respect and deep admiration forming from a shared experience of exclusion and discrimination. One woman passionately attracted to loving another woman while the other was forced to live within a culture that tried to wipe her own from the very earth itself. They recognized in each other similar gifts; endurance, persistence and the uncanny ability to defiantly face the threat of annihilation.

"I trust you," Angelique said softly. "What we are about to set into motion is going to kick open this viper's nest of poison."

"Yes. We'd better be prepared." Marti indicated the two women in the garden. "I hope they are strong enough for this."

"Our little deer has more courage than any of us," responded the taller woman. "The Creators are protecting her. We are the protectors Spirit has assigned. We will not fail."

Le Beau Jardin

The elegantly appointed office overlooked a central garden on the 7th floor of the Beau Jardin Hotel in Philadelphia. In addition to this location, Florida, the Bahamas and Manhattan, there was an exclusive villa in the hotel chain called Le Petite Beau Jardin on a private island. Anthony Tonhauer, owner and financier, sat at his antique walnut desk, gazing at reports from his management teams.

His phone buzzed, and he looked up from his reports. "Yes?"

"Mr. Holmes is here to see you."

"Thank you, Emily. Send him in and hold all calls for an hour."

"Yes, of course," was the soft reply.

The door opened and a large man entered the office. He was tall, tanned, and muscular. His expensive, custom made suit concealed the parts of his physique that were molded by years of extreme bodybuilding. Neither man extended their hand for a conventional handshake.

"Have a seat, Mr. Holmes."

The man sat down and his large frame filled the deep leather chair. "When we received your message, I decided to come myself."

"I'm glad you did. Is that courier business settled?"

"I can confirm the courier was dispatched. But it seems our employee hesitated. We instruct our staff to complete all assignments without observation. It turns out a motorist pulled over at a most inopportune moment. The employee evacuated the scene without completing the job."

"Was he reprimanded?"

"He was terminated," responded Holmes, "but the package has not been located yet."

"That's why I called the Agency." Tonhauer leaned back in his chair. "It seems Ms Norcross, my office manager at the kennel, received a call last week from a veterinarian in western New York. Somewhere by Lake Erie. Apparently, a couple months ago, an equine trainer brought in a microchip she found on the floor of her trailer after transporting some horses. She scanned it. It was one of ours. Ruby Tuesday."

Holmes lifted his eyebrows, causing deep lines to appear on his otherwise smooth forehead. "Why did the vet wait so long before contacting the kennel?"

Tonhauer shrugged. "She didn't think it was all that important at first. But then she thought maybe someone had stolen a show dog, removed the chip and just tossed in it an empty horse trailer. She figured knowing the chip had been found might be of interest to the kennel."

"There is no way the girl could have extracted that herself," he said.

"Correct. She had help."

"Shall I pay a visit to the vet?"

"Not necessary," said Tonhauer. "Norcross is very thorough. Here is the name and address of the horse stable. She easily acquired the information from the vet."

He handed the tall man a piece of paper with the handwritten words, 'Thunder Farms, Nadine Lawton, proprietor" and the address.

"I will take care of the matter myself, Mr. Tonhauer." He stood up.

"See that you do, Mr. Holmes."

Holmes left the office and Tonhauer quickly called his assistant.

"Emily, please have Mason at the airfield get the chopper ready. I will be going to the Little Mountain lodge today. I want to leave by six o'clock this evening. Please reschedule all my appointments. I will be gone for a week."

"Yes, of course," she responded.

He stood up and looked out the window toward the river.

"Yes," Tonhauer thought, "it's time for another retirement."

Marti Drops a Dime

Marti finished her cup of coffee and placed it on the desk. She sighed. This was no drive-through cup of coffee. It was an aroma rich, French-press, steeped and steaming cup of liquid pleasure. Jayne made the best; taking the time to grind the free trade, organic beans and steeping them in boiling water long enough for their distinctive flavor to emerge.

She glanced briefly at her notes. She did not want to be caught off guard. Picking up her smart phone, she pushed a smashed trac-phone off to the side.

Marti placed her call.

"Pennsylvania State Police, non-emergency line. How can I direct your call?" the disembodied male voice asked.

"This is Marti O'Neil, Philadelphia PD, retired," she stated with a flat voice. "I need to speak to the officer in charge of the Ice Mine Cut shooting. I have information regarding the investigation."

"Hold, please."

Several minutes later, a gravelly voice responded. "Lieutenant Abel Finch here. With whom am I speaking?"

"Marti O'Neil. Philadelphia Police, retired. I am a private investigator. I have information about the Ice Mine Cut shooting that occurred outside Lock Haven."

"And who said there was a shooting?" Finch responded, sounding bored.

"My witness."

That got his attention quickly.

"I need a name."

"I can give you a name, but I am pretty sure it's fake. However, the photo of the crime scene she texted me isn't."

"How did this person come to share this with you?"

"I got a call at my agency a few days ago. It was a woman who witnessed the shooting. She thought she was coming up to an accident. She started to call for assistance when she saw the man shoot the driver of the Camry."

Finch cleared his throat.

"The witness snapped a picture of the shooter instead. She texted me the photo and I will send it to you. She got a clear shot of the man and both vehicles with tags clearly visible."

"Why didn't she call 911 right away? Why wait nearly two months, then call a private detective?"

Marti had prepared for this line of questioning. She knew exactly what she would have asked in those circumstances.

"She was terrified he would kill her, too. She was afraid if she called the police, her name and address would become a matter of public record. I think she went into hiding at first in fear for her life. But she eventually called our agency, believing we would hold her identification confidential."

"Not in a murder investigation."

"Right. I can give you the cell number she called from and the name she gave me, but I doubt it's real."

"Try me."

"Marcia Davenport. It's a New York area code," Marti paused, then recited the number of the trac-phone on her desk.

"You said she texted you a photo."

'Yes. Do you want me to send it to you?"

"You can, but you need to come to the barracks and make a statement. Bring your phone, so I can verify the message, date and time stamp."

He gave her a number, and she texted back the photo that Angelique had taken. Marti felt her heart race with exhilaration, not fear. The familiar thrill of the moment when a troubled investigation broke wide open.

Finch inhaled sharply. Marti knew he had seen it.

"I took the witness's statement," she continued calmly. "Can I give it to you?"

"Yes, briefly. You can repeat it when you come here and then it will be official."

Yes, Marti thought, we are getting somewhere. Now for the tough part. She read from her notes, pausing to take a breath. She knew she was talking to a seasoned investigator who was cued to listen for inconsistencies.

"Ms. Davenport claims she was driving to Lock Haven on the morning of May 15th when she rounded the curve before the Ice Mine Cut. She saw a maroon Camry pulled off the road and a white Silverado truck half in the lane. She thought at first the truck stopped to help at the scene of an accident. She slowed down and took her cell phone out of its holder, meaning to call for assistance.

The truck driver had a gun. He shot the other driver, then looked up and saw her car. She snapped the picture at the point he holstered his firearm. He got in his truck and drove off.

The witness states, she then drove up to the Camry to see if the driver was still alive and need help. She saw the woman had been shot in the head and the inside of the car was strewn with items that looked like they had burst out of a cosmetic bag, which she saw lying on the floor. She states the victim was clutching a metal lipstick tube in her hand. She made a point of describing the victim's nail polish as a bright purple that stood out against the spatter of blood.

She then got in her car, spun around and drove back the way she came as fast as she could. She states she was in fear for her life. She felt she needed to leave the scene in case he came after her. She waited awhile before contacting a private investigation agency, believing it would afford her anonymity."

"That's all, sir," finished Marti.

"When can you come in to sign the statement and let me see your cell phone?"

"This afternoon."

"See you then, O'Neil," he responded.

Marti smiled as she terminated the call. "Not mam, like a regular citizen." She looked at her cell phone. She had deleted the security text app a few days ago. She would reinstall it later. All messages and photos Johanna had shared were also deleted.

She picked up the trac-phone. Before smashing it with a brick from the garden, she had erased all of its data. It would be tossed into a trashcan as she drove to the state police barracks. "Jayne," she called into the kitchen, "want to take a road trip?"

"Sure!"

"This time, I'm driving," Marti said as she put on her corduroy jacket.

"So that was your whole plan?" asked Jayne a short while later as they drove onto the Pennsylvania Turnpike ramp. She had been listening intently for the past twenty minutes as Marti relayed the details of her conversation with Abel Finch. "But how did you fake the phone call?"

"I bought the trac-phone with cash at that convenience store in Newburgh we stopped at after we left the Neptune Diner. Untraceable. I activated it with a made-up name and address. Then I forwarded Johanna's photo of the Ice Mine crime scene to the trac-phone. I deleted the photo from my cell that Johanna originally sent. I waited one day and then I called my cell phone from the trac-phone. I left an open line for half an hour, then ended the call. Then I texted the photo from the trac-phone to my cell, so it has a verifiable date and time stamp that correlates with the date I claimed I was called by the witness. "

"All the evidence on the trac-phone is deleted?" Jayne asked.

"Of course."

"Can I make the drop?"

"Sure," Marti replied, smoothly changing lanes. "There're plenty of plazas along the turnpike to choose from. The trac-phone is in a plastic bag in the console. Use the nitrile gloves. Drop it in a waste container when we gas up, not the gloves, though."

"You think of everything, don't you?"

"I try to." Marti grinned at Jayne, who returned the sentiment with a conspiratorial smile.

Hours later, Abel Finch escorted Marti out of the state police barracks office. He returned to the computer on which he had already run the plates on the Silverado. The owner, Tom Dresden, was dead, killed on the train tracks in Emporium. Not only did the photo from the witness show Finch's crime scene, the description of the victim was accurate, right down to her purple fingernails.

He picked up his phone and made a call to the Emporium state police barracks. It seemed Trace Helberg's suicide fatality had murdered his gunshot victim.

When Rivers Speak to Rivers

I t was dawn on the mountain. Johanna had just finished her morning yoga and meditation. Now that the weather was warm with the grace of midsummer, she completed her dawn practices in the garden. Her downward dog, cobra and sun salutation poses were accentuated by the rich, earthy smells of growing vegetables and the fragrant scent of companion flowers.

She sat in meditation by the lodge poles of the Three Sisters. Corn, the elder sister, grew tall on strong stalks, providing guidance and wisdom to the vines of pole beans that gently wound around them; the younger sister providing support. At the base, sweet butternut squash was planted, the youngest sister who gave protection and nourishment to her elder sisters. Each supported the growth of the others by providing different nutrients that enriched the soil. What one plant took from the soil, another returned. Johanna's meditation cushion was poised on a space of earth beside the lush, growing poles.

The scent of marigolds offered living incense for her practice. The drone of bees buzzing lazily by the orange squash blossoms was her meditation chant. As caretaker and harvester, she was placed in right relationship with the land. In that moment, she acknowledged she must give as much as she took from its revenues. For the abundant wealth of food and water, warmth and fresh air to continue unbroken, she must give back her own riches and gifts.

Angelique had taught her Spirit had hidden a gift within each human being. It was a very special medicine that needed to be discovered, cultivated, and given away without hesitation when the world needed it.

Humans needed clean water to drink, healthy food to eat, and fresh air to breathe. The earth embedded within her human children unique gifts to be traded for this natural goodness. This form of reciprocity was an eternal promise that needed to be honored in order for life to continue for all beings.

To believe you truly possessed your surroundings, to horde your gifts and never give back, was an unwholesome recipe for unimaginable destruction. Angelique taught her the western mind was plagued with the kind of hubris that caused them to steal the very things they needed to share, along with a false sense of unworthiness that prevented them from seeing the sacred within themselves.

Long ago Johanna had confided to her friend that she had born "under the veil," which her Scots grandmother had explained meant she had the Second Sight. She had been born while still within the sack of waters. She had also been told not to talk about her visions because it might be considered witchcraft. The cultural differences were extraordinary. What in her culture of origin was often deemed evil, indigenous cultures believed were powerful gifts from the Creators. The word 'shaman' itself meant a holy one.

"Your gift, Netuksq," said Angelique, "is to see things in a sacred way. You must learn to listen just as well so you can give away your gift in the way it is most needed." They had been walking near a creek many years ago when Angelique taught her these powerful truths. It was during the early years after graduate school, when they worked together at the women's center, that the first lessons took place. Johanna was beginning to use her abilities to enhance the counseling she provided to women who had fled dangerous relationships.

She was learning to combine western therapeutic skills with her gift of seeing. She was able to meet her clients right where they were, lost in a forest of confusion or blocked by the weight of trauma and abuse. Her gift allowed her to find each person in the very place they were lost and guide them back to healing and wholeness.

She saw what happened to them. Literally saw it. Even if a woman could not remember for fear of being overwhelmed, Johanna knew exactly what she had endured. A clinical supervisor in Johanna's training days had criticized her for using clairvoyance in therapy.

"You should know there is no place in this work for the paranormal," she had remarked with disdain. "Empathy and intuition are clinical tools, of course, but don't imagine you can actually know another person's experience."

Johanna was shaken by the encounter. She was considering leaving the training program altogether, believing herself unsuitable for doing this form of work. She could not stop seeing the images in her mind. Angelique had rescued her.

She introduced Johanna to the creek that was to become her wisdom teacher. Angelique told her she had learned long ago what European minds could tolerate knowing and what they couldn't.

"When you need to share your thoughts, when you have questions or need support in these matters, you need to bring your concerns to your spirit allies, not your clinical supervisor." Her sparkling laughter blended with the sound of rippling water that wound through the rocks of the creek bed.

"They, at least, know what to do with your gifts and will help you develop them. I, myself, know things because my spirit allies are always telling me things. But they don't show me. I can imagine that suddenly seeing things that actually happened to someone else would be disturbing. But that is exactly why you need to go into nature for your training. The journeys will teach you what you need to know and the actions you need to take. Your wisdom teachers will show you how to stay in balance. The shaman's path can drive a person crazy, you know."

They had come to a clearing where two streams joined together. Angelique unrolled a sleeping bag on the ground and told Johanna to lie down. She took a beautiful hand made, fringed shawl from her pack and covered Johanna.

"Close your eyes, Netuksq, and listen to my drum, my rattle, and the sound of the two streams talking to one another," she instructed. "They will answer your questions."

This had been Johanna's first shamanic journey. She learned she was an integral part of a more-than-human world. There were sky and underworld journeys which offered vastly different perspectives. This information usually came while the seeker was in an altered state of mind, created by drumming, not assisted or distorted by drugs. There were also middle world journeys that occurred in so-called real time. Johanna learned her gift of seeing was an extension of this kind of journeying.

When she was a young girl, Johanna loved to collect rocks. She was attracted to smooth rocks and crumbly worn rocks, striated stones and those with bands of shiny mica. She remembered each one of them as if they were personal friends. On a sunny day, she would put them in a bucket of water and give them a bath, thinking they missed the rain.

Her mother had suggested she show her box to a neighbor who was a retired geologist and lapidary, who now spent his time cutting and polishing gems. "I'm sure Dr. Milner can help you identify them." The thought that the rocks actually had names was exciting to Johanna.

The geologist not only helped her learn about the many forms of rocks and stones, but about the incredible earth forces that shaped them. She learned about the ancient formations of the Badlands of South Dakota and how the entire area was once the homeland of extinct creatures of over 33 million years ago, then inundated under a vast sea. Now it was a twisting mountainous region of eroding rocks, pinnacles, and striated bands with embedded fossilized bones.

"Imagine what those rocks, mountains, and stone canyons have seen throughout time," he told her. "What stories they could tell if they could speak?"

In the scheme of earth time, she learned, 33 million years was young compared to the arctic mountains of Greenland whose intense pressure over 3 billion years ago created rich veins of gem quality rubies and pink sapphires.

He handed her a large white stone shaped like a block. "Where do you think that came from?"

As she held it in her hands, she saw a tall building in her mind, many stories high, with stone steps and spires. "The building only has steps on three sides," she described, "but one side is built into a hill."

His breath caught in his throat. "This is a sandstone block from the site of Palenque in the Yucatan peninsula. I was working on a restoration in college years ago and brought it back with me. It was lying on the ground by a tall temple that was built into the side of a hill. How did you know that?"

What she didn't tell him was that the stone block had fallen from its holding place in the tower and had lain for a thousand years on the ground, longing to be a part of a revered structure again. It was lost now, stolen from its sacred ground. Johanna felt its immeasurable sadness. She had held it in her small hands and a tear slid from her eyes onto the limestone block. It was absorbed immediately, and she felt a sense of peace flowing throughout her body. This was the first of her many encounters with the more-than-human world.

She learned that rocks like to surface from beneath the soil over time or plunge from cliffs to rest in rivers and streams. They liked to move around, shift, change, or break apart. Sometimes it took a small seismic shudder to have an immediate result, other times it took a million years. Their time frame for consciousness was very different from humans.

She discovered in a journey that the kind of wisdom rocks and land wielded was very different from that of human beings. Having biological minds, her kind had thoughts and developed philosophies that included peace and harmonious relationships. The substances of earth; rock, sand, minerals, quartz, mountains and riverbeds had no thoughts whatsoever. Their entire beingness was defined by balance, order, and harmony. Even in the midst of volcanic eruptions and the incredible pressure and heat that created a diamond, there was the force of balance.

She imagined that the perspective of a billion year wisdom contained in a single stone whose only objective was keeping things balanced dwarfed any knowledge developed by human existence on the planet. She had no other way to describe the power of a shaman stone. It just was.

Angelique suggested Johanna come to the place by the two streams when she needed clinical supervision of a spiritual sort.

Over the years, Johanna returned many times and received a wealth of training that was available through no other means.

"They are always talking to one another," she shared with her mentor. "It's the splashing, that's humor and laughter, a soft bubbling sound that's crying and it's the flow that's the storytelling!"

Angelique had laughed over the phone when they spoke that day so many years ago. "They are full of stuff to share, aren't they?"

"When they dry up," remarked Johanna, "they need to hear your stories. You can fill them up again. Apparently, they love to hear what's going on."

"So true," Angelique had said. "Those little rocks and the big ones that have fallen into the riverbed are memory holders. Ancient wisdom embedded in the middle of a river that likes to tell stories is a real way to share knowledge, don't you think? Those stories travel all around the world. Rivers are big gossipers!"

It was a different river Johanna planned to visit on this day. After her morning gardening, she would go to the lower creek by the falls where she and Scott liked to hike. One of the most elegant spiritual truths she had learned years ago from the Two Streams was that rivers spoke to rivers.

By mid-morning, Johanna had left her car in the Kettle Creek parking area and settled her pack on her back. A bouquet of fragrant orange marigolds in her hand, she walked along the creek trail. The water was low in places and trickled its way through the rocks in the creek bed.

She saw a flat rock with two streams of water running on either side. "It's a two-stream," she thought, as a smile came to her face. "This is the place to ask." The creek bed was dry enough on its banks here; she could walk, hop, and finally land on the flat rock.

Johanna placed the bouquet on the rock, sat down, and closed her eyes, listening. The stream on the right was louder, not as deep as the faster stream on the left. They were two separate river voices conversing but taking no notice of the human perched on the boulder between them. She heard a plunking sound from an indiscernible direction and that was when she felt everything shift.

"Hello, old friends," she said aloud. "I have come to ask a favor. It's difficult. Is there an old one, a wise stone who is willing to travel to a new place, knowing it will never return to its million year home? To do ceremony and use its power to block bad intentions?"

She heard another plunk in the stream. She continued. "Children are being hurt and killed. I would ask the allies to assist, to empower this stone to become a shaman and battle the people harming these children."

She felt a little silly then, hearing her own voice, asking the river for guidance with the greatest humility she could muster. That's when she noticed how quiet it had become. The sound of birds in the forest had hushed. She felt the presence of spirit.

Words tumbling in her mind like a waterfall rushing into her heart. *Downstream*, the words said, *you will know the place*. And that was all. She left two of the marigolds on the rock and thanked this place of power for its guidance.

From her den on the ledge of the mountain, she felt the pull of power. It was like the scree of an eagle wailing in her mind. She rose and trotted through the forest, back slung low, head held close to the ground. She heard the thunder of the waterfall in the distance.

She could feel the tendrils of power singing through the trees beside her. She only needed to hunt along the path they wove to find her prey. The singing became louder as she came to the edge of the creek. The water below swirled in circles.

She extended her paw and playfully tapped the muddy bank like a cat trapping a mouse, then withdrew. Power was now rushing to this very place. She moved under the branches and crouched. She could no longer be seen.

One rainstorm and the flat rock would be submerged, the two streams becoming one, Johanna thought. They had known she was coming. Places of power move around, she thought as she stepped carefully over the rocks toward the trail.

Walk in the creek bed, by the edge. She heard the words flow through her mind. She saw an image of a rain bell, a rope with tiny copper bells tied to it. The kind people hung from a rain gutter. When it rains, it sings. So the two streams wished her to honor them that way. She would hang a rain-chain from a tree in her Medicine Buddha garden. She nodded as she walked along the inner edge of the creek bed.

Within a few minutes, she reached a place where an eddy of the river swirled to the edges of the creek. This was the place, but which stone wanted to be chosen? She sat down on a rock and looked into the clear water below. A leaf spinning on the eddy swirled into the little pool. She watched. She looked up on the riverbank and saw a paw print in the mud.

Fresh. A mountain lion was here not long ago. The human part of Johanna shivered and felt the urge to leave immediately. But the more than human part, her shaman eyes became a little sharper.

There was only one paw print. Not complete tracks. How is that possible? she wondered.

She leaned closer and as she shifted her position, the sun glinted off a stone in the bottom of the pool. The sparkle caught her attention, so she reached into the water.

It was a small stone that had been washed clean by flowing water. No marks, no special striations. Simple. Quite perfect.

While holding the stone in the palm of her hand, she felt the permission it was granting. She saw exactly how she was to paint it. She saw a blood red print of a small hand reaching out painted on its side. In her mind, she saw the shaman stone it would become.

Johanna left one marigold by the big cat paw print and scattered the rest in the eddy pool. She carried the little stone in her hand as she walked down the trail to her car.

Yes, she thought, when this river talks to other rivers, what a story it will tell. It will speak about a little wisdom gatherer stone that walked away to become a mighty shaman. She felt honored to be its transporter. When this phase of the ceremony was done, it would literally be out of her hands.

Her great heart skipped a beat as the woman walked away. This woman has humility. She is part of her surroundings. Her golden coat gleamed in the late afternoon sunlight as she crept down to the stream and sniffed the sharp musky scent of the flower offering. Yes, this one would be a great shape-shifter.

Her One True Name

It was a hot August day, and the sun rode high in a cloudless sky. Birds called to one another in the forest and the barn was busy. Nadine decided it was a beauty day. The farrier was coming to trim hooves. The stalls were fresh and clean. A truck was coming in late afternoon to haul away the manure pile.

Each horse would be led to the outdoor bathing stall and given a sudsy shower, then rinsed. Nadine would pick their feet first; inspecting their hooves and legs, assuring any potential infections would be caught early.

Ruby's job was to groom each and every horse thoroughly, brushing them out and combing manes and tails. Dirt and caked mud would be brushed off their backs and bellies, preparing them for the bath. It was dirty work, after which the barn floor would need a good sweep.

"Sam Red Deer and Fox are coming by to ride Merlin," said Nadine, "so start with him."

Ruby walked down to the paddocks with a lead rope to bring back the dark bay thoroughbred. He was another million-dollar horse like Stable Ticket. As long as he made money for his owners, he had value. As he aged, though still young in horse years, he became more a liability than an asset to his owners.

Nadine had told Ruby about the racing industry and how she rescued as many as she could. She ran a non-profit thoroughbred rehabilitation farm. Currently, there were six horses and room for three more.

"When we have a full house," Nadine had said, "Fox comes and helps out. But now that you are here, we might be able to expand."

Ruby passed Stable Ticket's paddock. He picked up his ears and watched her as she walked by. Merlin was in a lower field beyond Rampage and Willow, who grazed together. Stormcatcher, the dappled thoroughbred and Aqueneh stood together munching from a pile of hay Nadine had left in each paddock earlier as she made her rounds in the hay cart.

She would have to duck under the fence to catch Merlin. Most of the horses on the farm came willingly when they saw her coming with the bright blue lead rope. But Merlin liked to run away.

She had tried a different color rope, no go. It was a game with him. She rummaged in her pocket for a treat. Walking through the open field, she meandered over to where Merlin was yanking up some clover.

The smell of clover was sweet, and she wished she could take off her muck boots and walk barefoot in the field. She reached down and pulled up a bunch of clover. Holding it out, she approached the horse, who looked at her warily.

He snorted and then dashed to the back of the paddock, kicking up dust devils from his hooves. She turned around and started to walk away. She could sense his interest perking up. He started to walk toward her, curious. She hummed a tune she remembered from long ago.

She could only remember a few words and a glimmer of the face of an older woman singing her to sleep. *"..... coming for to carry me home...."* she had sung. The tune was repetitive, and remembering it had brought her comfort later when she had slept on the cot in her kennel cage.

She stopped suddenly in the field and dropped the clump of clover. The woman was her grandmother from Jamaica. But she hadn't been able to protect her after all. Memories flooded back into her mind. She had lived with her grandmother on the island of Jamaica when she was little. Her mother had come to America to find a better way of life. She came for her one day and brought her back to this land.

She wasn't kind like her grandmother. She had sold her to the Kennel and left her there. Her body began to shake and her heart raced so hard she thought it would burst. Her mind froze into emptiness.

She was standing as still as a statue when Merlin suddenly nudged her. He had walked up behind her without her being aware of his presence. He snorted and his hot breath spilled over her shoulder. She could feel the steady beat of his great heart as he stood motionless behind her. Her heartbeat began to match his, softly at first, then strong and powerful. The fear slipped away and was replaced with an inexplicable calmness.

She turned and offered a treat with one hand, took his halter and clipped on the lead rope. Once caught, he followed her to the gate. As she led him up the hill, she wondered if Nadine could really keep her safe.

Passing by Willow and Rampage, she thought a new name meant no one could hurt them anymore. Maybe a new name would make her safe, too.

Minutes later, she put Merlin on the cross ties in the barn.

"What kept you?" Nadine asked, "Merlin being tricky again?"

The girl nodded, getting the brush box from the tack room. She had retreated back into the silence of her mind. Nadine could feel it.

She respected the girl's need to feel safe and to work in silence. She also knew focusing on caring for these creatures was healing for both the horses and the child. She inspected Merlin's feet as she picked out clumps of dried mud.

By the time the farrier arrived, the other horses had been brushed out and were waiting for a turn in their stalls. Ruby led Rampage to the wash stall. Nadine had a fresh bucket of warm, soapy shampoo prepared. Ruby tied his lead rope to the iron ring on the outer wall of the barn.

"How did he get the name Rampage?" she asked. "He is so calm and good natured. He never acts up."

Nadine laughed. "A horse's true name comes from something unique about them. It's something that gives away a secret. I believe it's the name The Creators know them by, so we have to watch and wait for the name to show up."

She used a loofah sponge to cleanse his back and legs before hosing him down. The horses loved the feel of the water spraying them, adjusted for comfort by the warm and cold handles of Nadine's barn faucet.

"I think they remember being colts and fillies in a field during rainstorms. The spray from the hose is like warm rain to them," Nadine said.

Rampage arched his head to the sky as Nadine sprayed him down, flooding the soapy water from his neck. She stepped back to let Ruby use the squeegee to remove the excess water from his coat.

"Have you ever noticed," asked Nadine, "his stall is always the worst to clean? Most horses are aware enough to keep their hind end in the same place in a stall," she laughed, "but not him."

Nadine's laugh was contagious. Most of the time, she was a serious woman not usually given to jokes or lightheartedness. But when she laughed, it was like a field of lightning bugs on a summer night. It was like someone magically turned on fairy lights in the middle of the darkness.

"He sure makes a big mess," said Ruby. "He knocks his feed bucket off the wall and kicks it around the stall, then rolls in the straw."

"He used to be a cribber and chew the wood on the stall door. It is a bad habit and hard to correct. But he never does those things when you are there to see it. Fox said it's like he goes on a rampage during the night, but no one hears it. "

"So he got called Rampage?"

"Yes. His race name was Warrior's Son. See how his true name reveals a secret," Nadine continued. "Willow's race name was Lady of Grace. If you watch her in the paddock, she sways back and forth like a willow tree. She does the best serpentines of any thoroughbred I have ever trained. She bends. She is a great dressage horse."

"You know about Merlin. He's tricky and he can do anything from dressage to eventing. But in his heart, he is a jumper. That's why I will only sell him to a rider who wants to jump him."

"What if someone offered more money to event him?" Ruby asked.

Nadine shook her head. "That wouldn't be fair to Merlin."

"What about Stormcatcher and Aqueneh?" Ruby asked.

"Stormcatcher's name was Zeus when he raced. He is also up for sale. Now he is truly an eventer. An eventer needs to be able to jump over different obstacles. He needs stamina and agility to make quick turns and run fast on open ground. He must be able to swim. He must have what we call ride-ability."

"When he was in his first event," Nadine continued, "there was a thunderstorm in the middle of the cross-country run. Most of the horses were afraid and hard to control, so their riders had to bring them in. But Stormcatcher did not seem to mind the thunder and lightning. He was able to finish the cross country course before coming in from the rain."

"But Aqueneh is special to me. She was called Silent Whisper when she came to me about ten years ago, so she is about eighteen now. She is a Paint, a rare color for a thoroughbred, dark smoky charcoal and white. She is a wise horse, the lead mare around here. I had just lost my daughter, Josette. My heart was not in rescuing horses anymore. I was ready to sell the farm."

"Is Nadine your true name?" Ruby asked.

"No, Thunderchild was given to me many years ago by an elder. It means fearless. Aqueneh means peace. After Josette was taken, I thought I would die. But that horse reminded me of who I truly was. She helped me find peace again. I will never sell her."

"Come, let me show you something," said Nadine gently. She led Aqueneh out to the riding ring with only a halter and lead rope. Ruby followed.

In the ring, Nadine boosted the girl onto the thoroughbred's bare back. "Hold on to that tuft of mane at the base of Aqueneh's neck. Let your legs and toes hang down because there are no stirrups. This is how my people rode horses."

Ruby settled on the horse's broad back, holding the mane cautiously, and let her feet dangle around Aqueneh's wide belly.

"Now feel your thighs, your seat, and close your eyes. As Aqueneh walks, feel your body."

The girl held the mane tightly and let her body sway naturally from side to side as the horse slowly walked forward.

"That's right," Nadine said as she unclipped the lead rope and walked ahead of Aqueneh. The horse followed her.

"What do you feel?"

"My shoulders tingle," responded the girl.

"Can you feel her shoulders move as she walks? She feels the land through her hooves and the energy that rises from the earth. She knows the earth is her Mother, and that energy is rising through her legs and into yours. That energy is the love of Mother Earth for all her children. It is rising into your shoulders."

"I can feel it," said Ruby with excitement in her voice. "It's like a buzzing."

"Hang on." Nadine snapped her fingers and Aqueneh began to trot. "No posting, seated trot."

"Now, what do you feel?"

Nadine moved to the center of the ring and the horse began to trot in an ever-widening circle.

"The tingling moved to my hips! Side to side, matching her front legs hitting the ground."

"Aqueneh has a gift she is sharing with you. It is called 'good medicine,' said Nadine. "Not all medicine needs to be edible. Knowledge is good medicine that helps the people remember their true Mother is the earth. We are all related through her."

Nadine called out to Aqueneh, "Heyah, heyah!"

The horse's front legs rose up as she bounded upward into a rolling canter. Ruby hung on to Aqueneh's mane yet relaxed her body as she rolled with the movements of the horse. Her young body rose up and down with the horse's chest as the circle widened even more.

"Oh! I feel it in my heart! My heart thumps every time she pounds the ground!"

"That's right! Aqueneh is sharing her medicine wisdom with you. The earth is your Mother as well. She loves you. She gave you life and when you pass away, it is into her heart you will return. There is nothing to fear."

"Every child of Mother Earth has medicine knowledge to share and you do too," Nadine called out.

"But I don't know what it is!"

"Neehaaah…" called Nadine, lowering her voice as Aqueneh slowed down to a walk.

Ruby opened her eyes and looked at the native woman sadly. "Maybe I don't have any medicine."

"We will find it, child."

Later that afternoon, Sam Red Deer and his son drove into the stable yard in a black pickup truck. Nadine and Sam stood at the gate to the training ring while Ruby and Fox tacked up Merlin.

They had put the jumps in place. Fox led the thoroughbred into the ring and mounted him.

Ruby watched as Fox and rode Merlin around the ring, through the walk, trot and canter. She watched even more closely as Fox set Merlin up for a jump, then the horse took the air, his front legs tucked up to his chest. Horse and rider became wingless fliers again and again.

Fox could sense Merlin jumped as if his life depended on it. Not because he feared death, but because in his heart jumping was the freedom he lived for. The two were made for each other. Fox nodded to Sam as he dismounted. He handed Merlin's reins to Ruby and approached Nadine.

Nadine smiled. "So how would you like to train him a bit," she asked Fox. "I need a horse to compete for the barn in a show or two. I want to demonstrate what we can do here. If you take over his training and enter a few jumping shows, I will take down his price for you."

"I like that deal," responded Fox.

Sam Red Deer nodded.

That evening Ruby and Nadine sat on the farmhouse porch finishing a meal of fresh steamed corn and grilled steaks. Soon, they would close down the barn for the night and hand out the honor treats. The stars were just beginning to show themselves, sparkling centers of light that showed the glittering trails of the ancestors.

"We need to get up early tomorrow, child," said Nadine. "Ceremony at sun rise."

"Ok," responded the girl.

"You are being given your one true name. The name Spirit has been calling you every day to remind you who you really are."

The girl looked into Nadine Thunderchild's gentle face.

"Dawn?" she asked.

Nadine nodded.

"I feel it here," the girl said, holding her hand over her heart.

She Stalks Her Prey

The Pleiades glittered in the shadowed curve of a quarter moon. It was low in the sky. Known to indigenous people as the Seven Sisters, this constellation was setting in the west well before dawn. The Milky Way spread throughout the still night sky. Johanna gently kissed the husband of her heart as she left their bed.

Dressed and ready for the drive to Eastville, she would arrive by midday. She had booked a cabin at the Wandering Elk Campground about half an hour from Little Mountain. She quietly closed and locked the kitchen door, then drove out along the northern side of their land.

The Pleiades had ridden high in the summer sky all night. By the time she had driven to the mountain road, it had lowered below the horizon line. The Sisters were traveling to the western hemisphere where they would rise in the evening sky. Morning in the east was night on the other side of the world. All Her children needing guarding throughout the night so She placed the stars accordingly.

The road wound around tight turns, steep elevations that suddenly plunged down the mountainsides. Her headlights flashed into the woods as she rounded the corners and she focused intently for the sparkling reflections of animal eyes by the roadside. She would travel south for a few hours before connecting with the main highway, Route 80.

When she got to the highway, she would drive east, meandering through small townships in the mountainous wilds of Pennsylvania. Johanna generally loved road trips, but this one carried an element of danger she had purposely not shared with Scott when she told him about the trip.

She planned to drive past the campground to a fire road that ran behind the kennels. She wanted to scout the area as she planned to return under cover of night on unfamiliar roads. Throwing a shaman stone was itself an act of power. It needed to be placed in plain sight but to be unnoticeable to human eyes. In the sense that most people paid little attention to rocks and stones, this seemed somewhat easy. But shaman stones were decorated, painted, or adorned in a way that clearly set them apart from ordinary rocks.

One of the shaman tasks she had achieved in years past was the art of passing unnoticed through a crowded space. While that might seem an easy thing to do, it was actually harder than one might think. It's one thing to walk down a city street and have no one take notice of you, Johanna had explained to a friend who was interested in shamanism. But it's quite another to walk into a room occupied with people you know and pass through without being seen. She had honed her practice of silent walking during years of employment at The Glen.

She had successfully attended employee meetings and guest lectures at which her presence was not even noticed. As she drove through the college town of Lock Haven, she recalled a time one of her colleagues had asked her where she had been all day. They had actually passed one another in the spa hallways several times, but he never saw her. She had also attended one of his lectures, sitting quietly in the back of the room and smuggling herself out at the end, hidden in a throng of attendees.

Johanna smiled. She knew that had been a mastery of the skill of being unseen. People's brains are wired to recognize familiar faces, particularly when they are in anxious settings. This colleague always enjoyed having people he knew in attendance, as it made it easier for him to speak to his audience. She was there all along and he never noticed her.

This ability to use impeccable skills to enter an opponent's territory undetected and mark that space with an unseen force gives the shaman a kinetic influence. It interferes with an established pattern of energy and inserts powerful forces that result in a desirable change of outcomes. One never knew what might happen or how.

The powerful force Johanna would be introducing was ancient and wise. As she located this force in plain sight, it would be like her presence in the lecture, unseen. Who cares about rocks and stones in a gravel driveway or under a bush, she thought. How the stone would use its elemental wisdom to restore balance, she could not begin to guess.

By the time Johanna circled back to the campground, she was weary, but she had clearly determined the exact route to her destination. An easy in and out, she thought. She checked into the camp office at Wandering Elk and got the keys to her cabin. She brought in a cooler of food and lay down on the bed to rest. It was mid afternoon and her trip to the kennel would take place in the late evening, after hours.

At eight in the evening, she rose from the bed and refreshed her face with cool water from the faucet in the small bathroom. Changing into black jeans and t-shirt with a black hooded sweatshirt, she attached her hiking compass to her wrist and placed the stone in her back pocket.

She tucked her Sig Sauer pistol, with a bullet in the chamber and the safety on, in her concealed carry holster and wedged it in the front of her pants. She fitted her hiker's headband flashlight around her neck, rather than her forehead. Hands free, she could turn it on or extinguish it quickly. In the night, her darkly garbed figure was invisible. But sound mattered. Her black sneakers were soundless on pavement, but snapping twigs and crunching pebbles were audible giveaways. Other skills would be required to cloak her advance through the woods behind the kennels. Johanna carried a plastic bag with dog treats just in case she needed to toss more than a stone to complete her mission.

Half an hour later, she had turned onto the fire road then dimmed her vehicle lights. Turning the Subaru around for a quick escape if needed, she gathered her key fob and placed it in her other back pocket. She turned off the overhead light, which automatically illuminated when she approached the vehicle so even her car would remain darkened.

Heavy clouds concealed the quarter moon; not even a sliver of its reflection pierced the sky. When she closed the car door, she was immediately plunged into velvet black darkness. She touched her finger to the button on the flashlight around her neck and a pool of light appeared.

Johanna had positioned the vehicle by one of the narrow walking trails she had noticed on the Google Earth map that connected the back of the kennel to the fire road. Dog walkers from the kennel must have created those access paths to exercise the Salukis.

This made her objective much easier as the opening to the trail beside the Subaru was easy to locate. She pulled the hood over her head and instinctively bent forward as she walked along the trail.

She stopped for a moment and switched off the flashlight. She stood still and listened to the sounds of the night surrounding her. She felt a tightening around the edges of her eyes as if the skin was stretching. Her breath, as in a meditation, became slow and deliberate. Her fingertips tingled and her awareness circled down through her body and settled on the bottoms of her feet.

She felt the shift, though, into what she could not say. Her eyes adjusted to another source of illumination, not of human design. Her breath exhaled in little snorts and she began to walk. Not as a person who was intent on a purpose, but as Angelique had taught her, on the balls of her feet. Utterly silently, she walked. She became an imperceptible presence.

A soft light emanated from the energy of sap running in the trees and illuminated her way. Their branches glimmered against the obsidian darkness of the sky with a pale white glow. She moved forward slowly, crouching as she walked. The forest felt different now that she was a seamless part of it.

Her vision was enhanced as she began to see the world through more than human eyes. Her mind shifted. She was no longer a protector; she was, herself, a predator. What kind, she could not say. The self-awareness so distinctive in the human species had disappeared. She just, simply, was.

Ahead, beyond the fenced perimeter, a bright spotlight hurt her eyes. She continued, highly aware of the possibilities of human presence. Yet she did not sense anyone.

Before her was a chain-link fence surrounding the perimeter of the kennel yard. The top had an electrified wire. It was too high for a dog to leap over, but a painful deterrent for anyone attempting to get in. She had not considered this.

The human part of her realized it was also a deterrent to escaping, and then she knew where the girls were being held. She could see a series of cabins and a long building with attached wired cages for the Saluki show dogs.

The predator part of her felt her vision narrowing and her upper body flexing as if she was preparing to leap over the fence. She began to shift her balance from left foot to right foot as if her hind end was moving side to side, tightening the muscles in her thighs. In that moment, she only wanted one thing.

She wanted to take down her prey with a swift bite of her powerful jaws to their vulnerable, cowardly necks. She breathed heavily. Then something caught her attention.

A soft vibration in the left back pocket of her jeans reminded her who and what she was, a courier for Spirit. This stone had a job to do, and it refused to be distracted by a shaman who was becoming too enamored by the mystery of spirit ways.

She took the stone out of her pocket and took a last look at the blood red hand painted on its smooth surface. A force to be reckoned with, without a doubt, Angelique had said when Johanna showed it to her. It was an image similar to painted red ocher hand prints left on the walls of the Temple of Tulum. Thousands of women, over time, had come to the low stone shrine to petition the Mayan goddess for safe childbirth and medicine to heal their wounds. Not once had She failed to answer their needs. This stone carried the power of that feminine force. A small packet with a big punch, Angelique had said.

A moment before Johanna tossed the stone over the electrified fence, she wondered how that force could help the girls who were forced into sexual slavery. She knew this was an unpredictable, non-ordinary reality that could provoke dramatic and lethal results. Her heritage had no explanation for these types of influences. In fact, they were probably more effective because people with her ancestry didn't believe power like this even existed. It was hard to wrap your mind around, even for Johanna.

But then, one had to be in right relationship with the land for these mysterious forces to notice you at all. She let go of any thought she was responsible for what was about to happen. That was the final job of the courier. To fling the stone into a place that it would not be noticed, to walk away and not look back.

And that is exactly what she did. The stone landed with a soft plop by the back of one of the outbuildings. There was silence in the kennel yard. There was only the creak of the wind playing in the limbs of trees behind her in the forest.

She turned and walked back along the narrow trail toward the fire road. Deeper in the forest, she turned on her flashlight as her eyes had softened. There was no longer any light illuminating from the trees. If it were not for her flashlight, she would not have found her way back.

Johanna got in her car and drove back to the campground. She planned to leave the cabin at first light. What was set in motion was already beginning. What would be would be.

The Balls Start to Roll

Trace headed to the Lamar State Police station to meet Abel Finch. They both belonged to Troop F; but her station was located in Cameron County and his was in Clinton County. Dresden's autopsy report was in her briefcase on the seat of her vehicle. She needed to review the Webster autopsy report.

She chose the longer route to the Lamar station. It would take her past the Ice Mine Cut. She wanted to see the scene for herself. She would recognize it from the photo Finch texted to her.

Seeing the Silverado in one piece was impressive, she thought. Recognizing Dresden was another matter entirely. She had to rely on comparing his license image with the photo of the man at the Ice Mine Cut. So he had a firearm three days prior to his death. He owned a SIG Sauer P226 Legion pistol according to the gun registration she had located. The weapon had not been found in the truck or in his apartment. Troublesome, she thought.

Dresden did not kill himself, of that she was sure. There had been Rohypnol in his tox workup, enough to indicate he was completely incapacitated at the time of his death. He clearly could not have driven himself onto the train tracks. This was now a murder investigation.

The report stated his body showed scars from old knife and gun-shot wounds as well as a mended broken right hand. The medical examiner stated it was a boxer break, likely resulting from a fight. He suggested a stint in the army could explain the kind of wounds he was seeing, the kind you got in hand-to-hand combat. Trace tended to agree; she had a few scars like that of her own.

She has also learned Thomas Dresden has been employed by the Guardian Security Agency as a bodyguard. She had dug a little deeper and discovered the agency's client list. There were some interesting celebrities and not a few politicians in the mix. Sure, Dresden could have been former military. She was waiting for confirmation from the US Army and the Marines for his service record, if one existed. However, he did have another record. He had multiple assault charges that had all been dropped by the District Attorney's office. Curious.

Honorable discharge or otherwise, many soldiers opted for private security details after leaving the service. Trace ran her fingers through her short red hair; an action that often helped her stay focused. Given the choice, she had preferred law enforcement. There were some soldiers who no longer found killing distasteful. Perhaps the restraint prior to entering the military had been thin to begin with. She had met men and women like that while on active duty.

Trace Helberg was no stranger to killing, and she had learned to live with some deeply haunting memories. She dealt with them as a necessary price for her continued membership in the human race.

When she had looked at the unmarred face of Thomas Dresden in his license photo, she recognized a characteristic dullness in his eyes. There were those who killed to defend, and those that killed without remorse or conscience. Thomas Dresden had not been haunted by his memories.

She tilted the SUV's rear-view mirror down. Shiny blue eyes gazed back at her. You can't lose that, she thought. Ever.

All of her attention then shifted to driving as she descended the mountainous elevations, rounding sharp, tight curves. To her left, the West Branch of the Susquehanna swept lazily along the roadside. She came around a tight bend and instinctively slowed. The craggy, tall rock cliffs of the Ice Mine Cut lurched upward on the right. She saw the narrow turn off that was visible on the crime scene photo. She pulled the SUV off the road.

Crime scenes often still "spoke" long after they were cleared. She wanted to listen. Fifteen minutes later, Trace drove away. This bend in the road was a perfect place to ambush someone.

At Lamar, Lieutenant Abel Finch greeted her. He was an old dog of a trooper, sixty-ish, grey-haired and paunchy. He gripped her hand like an iron rod and thrust a paper-cup of coffee at her. She returned his handshake with one of her own. It was the one that had earned her the nickname "Valkyrie" in the service.

Upon returning home from active duty, she had told her parents about the nickname she received. Her father's blue eyes twinkled when he grinned. "That's no surprise to me."

Her mother, an Icelandic woman who ancestors were Norsemen as well, said softly, "It fits. The Valkyrie decided who lived and who died on the battlefield."

Her height had something to do with that reputation as well. At six feet, many men had to look up to meet her icy blue gaze. Unusual in a woman, but then Trace Helberg was unusual in many ways. For as long as she could remember, she stood out as different in a crowd.

She had beaten up her first bully in a sixth-grade school yard. A schoolboy had pushed a younger girl down in the dirt. As he turned around to a cheering group of fellow boys, Trace sucker punched him in the nose and he landed in the dust. His cheering squad then laughed at him and the school principal thought that humiliation by his peers and a detention was punishment enough. She got off with an admonishment that fighting boys was unseemly for a girl. If only he knew, she remembered thinking at the time. She didn't see much difference between genders and believed cruelty was never acceptable.

She considered her height, strength and agility as skills that needed refinement. At the University of Colorado, she joined the rifle team and the chess club. Her height and lower center of gravity, as well as her single-minded focus, contributed to her sharp shooter status.

She competed in cross-country skiing, where her impressive longer stride was a key factor in her performance. Chess was a mind game in which she had honed the ability to strategize five steps ahead of her opponents. She had the reputation of unnerving teammates with her piercing stare. She mastered the art of losing with the same silent, unemotional grace as her wins.

"Follow me. You can use my system," Finch said gruffly. "You have the autopsy report on my killer, right?"

"Yes, I'd like to see the Webster autopsy report. Can I read your witness statement as well?"

"Let me sum it up for you," Finch swung open his office door and pointed to an old swivel chair behind the desk. "It will save you some time."

"My vic, Elaine Webster, was shot and killed by a single gun shot to the face. Died instantly. 9mm bullet fragments were recovered, hollow point, maximum damage. She was no innocent lady. Multiple prior charges included both prostitution and procurement, all conveniently dropped. Employed by the Little Mountain Saluki Dog Kennels.

"A hit," said Trace, "but why?"

Finch shrugged his shoulders.

"Contents of the vehicle included a handbag, suitcase, two passports. There was one for her and one for an eighteen-year-old girl, Rosalita Martinez. Oh and yeah, a cosmetic bag with enough makeup to paint a team of whores was strewn all over the floor by the front passenger seat. Purple nail polish on her fingers, toes, and a few bottles of the stuff on the floor."

"Where was her handbag found?" Trace asked. "Not bad." She held up her coffee.

He consulted his report. "Back seat. Floor."

"Crime scene photos?"

Finch pushed a report folder across the desk toward her. "All yours."

She looked through the gruesome pictures. He watched her face, waiting for the response of a rookie new to the visceral shock of violent death. Her face did not register any response.

Cold, he thought to himself.

"I find it odd her handbag is here in the back of the car and her makeup case is beside her," she stated. "She is run off the road. A man points a gun at her and she is rummaging for make-up."

"Who knows why a woman does what she does?" stated Finch.

"Was she reaching for a weapon?"

"None found. And the witness report states he did not enter the vehicle, so he did not remove one."

"I will need to see that." Trace traded the folder with Dresden's autopsy report for the anonymous witness statement.

She glanced back at the crime scene photos of Elaine Webster. She had two passports; she had a suitcase. She was running, Trace thought. Where is the girl?

"I need to visit the evidence locker. I want to know what she thought was so important right before she was shot."

Finch shrugged. "Sure."

She picked up the witness statement.

"Oh, yeah, final autopsy note," Finch stated casually.

Trace looked up.

"There was a micro chip planted in her shoulder. The examiner dug it out and scanned it. Vet chip, registered to Little Mountain Dog Kennels with the name "Fast Lane.""

Trace looked shocked. Finch smiled to himself. Got cha.

"Follow me," he said.

The evidence room was at the end of a hallway in a separate wing of the building. They signed into the evidence room log. Finch located the boxes containing Elaine Webster's personal effects, and the contents found in her car.

"I'll leave you to it," he said as he backed away from the flat wooden table in the middle of the evidence holding room.

"No, please stay," Trace held up her hand, as intuitive flashes burst in her brain like the itchy warnings that prevented her from stepping on land mines.

"No reason to," he responded. "My case is closed."

"I said, stay," Trace said. Her eyes flashed and her voice had the edgy sharpness of one used to commanding others. For a moment, she was a captain again in a field of battle. Finch's startled look brought her back to the present. Her rank was far below Finch's senior position.

She dropped her gaze. "I may need you to interpret some of this evidence. My case is still open and I believe the reason Dresden killed Webster is the reason he was murdered as well. The more I know about your victim," she continued, "the more I will learn about mine."

Finch pulled a metal chair from the side of the room and sat down with an amused expression on his face.

Donning a pair of white nitrile gloves, Trace started with the clothing, removing a large plastic bag from the box. Blood spattered blue jeans, a cheap belt and a dark blue sweater with dried brain matter stuck to it. Brown socks and old-fashioned loafers. Underwear was white cotton with a blood-soaked bra, standard Walmart 'Cross Your Heart' with wide elastic shoulder straps.

She put the clothing back into the bag. She then looked through the box containing the clothing removed from the suitcase. More drab apparel. Not even a racy nightgown, flannel for God's sake, she thought. No teenager's clothing. It's like she held up the corner thrift store before leaving town.

"To a prostitute," she remarked to Finch, "this clothing is the equivalent of camouflage. She was on the run. He was sent to stop her."

"Why," he responded, "there isn't anything there."

"Maybe it's not what she had, but what she knew?"

He shrugged and looked up at the paint peeling off the ceiling.

She opened a plastic bag with the blood spattered cosmetic case and dumped the contents onto the table. She recalled the witness statement and the crime scene photos all at once, like the tableau of an operation, a sortie. The images coalesced like an attack mission coming together in her mind. This was not a random cosmetic bag a woman had put together with her favorite cosmetic items. There would be mixed brands of make-up. This was a professional make-up kit.

One brand. Chaude au Coeur. She pulled the crumpled cosmetic company brochure from the pile on the table and scanned it. Why have a brochure in your makeup kit? she mused. She lined up three bottles of purple nail polish and one large, bullet shaped tube of lipstick. The bottoms of each container read, "Fast Lane." The same as the name on the vet chip, a dog at a kennel, she thought, the same color as the victim's fingernails.

Trace crouched down, lowering her face to the level of the table top and viewed her line up at eye level. Why did Webster need this much nail polish and only one tube of lipstick? She retrieved the photo of Elaine Webster. As bloody as she was and from what remained of her face, the woman had clearly not been wearing purple lipstick.

She looked up to see Finch staring at her intently.

"The witness report stated Elaine Webster was clutching a lipstick tube, this one," Trace said. "The only one in the bag. The crime scene photo showed that her hands were empty."

"Yeah, so…" Finch responded. His eyes glinted with interest as he struggled to follow her line of reasoning.

Then Trace Helberg did what any other woman would have done. She opened the tube and rolled up the lipstick, expecting to see a blob of purple gloss. A very small metal flash-drive popped up. It just barely fit in its hiding place. She removed it with nitrile-covered fingers.

"Your case, your jurisdiction," she said, holding it up to the florescent lights.

"Let's add it to the evidence roster, dust it for prints and open it up," Finch said. "Something tells me we just hit the jackpot. How are your tech skills? Do we need a specialist?"

"I can do it."

"You're good," Finch said, with admiration.

"There are two reasons they call me Trace and none of them is short for Tracy," she said. "I focus on all the details, leave no trace unexplored. And tracer beams in the night give me migraines."

And that is how Abel Finch learned the Valkyrie was no rookie.

Hours later, with the ravaged remains of a pizza box tossed on an old wooden chair, Trace was still hunched over the computer monitor on Finch's desk. The flash drive had been inserted into the port of his PC.

The one-terabyte hard drive was disappointing. It contained dog show photos. She had just viewed every single one. Trace thought, why would anyone store this small amount of data on a stick with this amount of capacity then hide it in a lipstick tube?

Human nature never ceased to surprise her. People, it seemed, were not only complicated, she thought, they were strange. All her life, she had tried and failed to blend in. Eventually, she turned her lack of success in being accepted into a superior skill of analyzing human behavior.

When you don't belong, she learned, you could be extraordinarily objective. You won't miss details others take for granted. This ability and being a consummate chess strategist gained her a certain kind of reputation in the military. When she mounted an operation, there were fewer casualties and more intel was gathered.

In the case of a data drive hidden in a lipstick tube, Trace was relentless. You can't access what you can't see, she thought. She pulled a directory of files, using system commands outside the windows environment. The cold, pale light of the monitor cast an eerie illumination across her face. Finch slept while leaning back in a swivel chair taken from a colleague's office. His feet were propped up on the desk that Trace was hunched over.

The directory list scrolled down the screen. The drive had one terabyte of capacity. One hundred sixty-three gigabytes were used and eight hundred thirty-seven gigabytes were free. Thirty-six gigabytes of the used space were in image files, the dog show photos. But there were nearly one hundred twenty-seven gigabytes in hidden sectors. These were not viewable without a password.

She knew how to get around that. A few quick keys strokes later, she had used a command code structure to rename the drive designation, labeled it viewable and opened it.

She saw a directory labeled Saluki Film Productions. She clicked on it, revealing another directory named 'auditions.'

She clicked again.

There were three more directories labeled 'Rosa Linda,' 'Fast Lane,' and 'Ruby Tuesday.' She opened an mp4 video labeled Rosa Linda and watched for about three minutes.

Trace sat back, stunned.

"Finch!" she slammed the table. "We've got 'em by the balls!"

Abel Finch woke with a jolt.

Sugarcamp Road

Nadine had developed a strict training routine for Stable Ticket that capitalized on the racehorse's attraction to Dawn. Their relationship went far beyond treats and mutual affection.

Each day, in midafternoon, Dawn would bring Stable Ticket in from his paddock on a lead rope. In the barn she would put him on the crossties and groom him, pick his hooves, then saddle him. She would lead him out to the riding ring for lunging and training with Nadine.

Afterwards, Dawn was in charge of brushing out and giving him a treat. This way, his treats were directly related to his ring performance. As time went on, Nadine planned, she would see if he would accept the evening honor treat from her along with the other horses after night feeding.

This routine was working well with both girl and horse, seeming to gain confidence daily. Nadine was pleased with their accomplishments. Stable Ticket was performing well under saddle as she trained him in serpentines and simple equitation. Dawn excelled in her grooming and riding, never seeming to fear these huge creatures.

It was a warm day with a cloudless sky. The forest was full of cicadas singing, woodland birds chirping and flying across the paddocks. Nadine had just completed training Rampage, who was becoming expert over the trot poles. As she led him into the barn for brushing out, she passed Dawn, leading Stable Ticket to the riding ring.

The girl walked the racehorse across the farmyard on his lead rope and halter, his bridle slung over her shoulder. He nudged her pockets, knowing she carried his treats. Nadine had left the lunge line on a fence post in the riding ring for the next phase of their routine.

As she brushed out Rampage, Dawn lunged Stable Ticket in the ring. Now an active part of his training, the girl was learning how to manage and care for all the horses.

After Nadine put Rampage in his stall, she walked over to the gate at the ring. That was Dawn's signal to bring the racehorse to the fence, where she would remove his halter and put on his bridle. Stable Ticket dropped his head for her to make the change and easily took the bit as she secured the bridle straps on his head. As a daily routine, he complied each time willingly, without balking or moving away. Dawn handed Nadine the reins and left the ring.

Nadine tightened the girth and slid the stirrups down. Though she was a very tall woman, she needed the mounting block to ride this racehorse. In the saddle, she gathered the reins and in her mind formed the thought, "forward." She leaned very slightly, and he began to walk forward.

Dawn watched from the gate, studying Nadine's seat, hand movements and other signals. Most were imperceptible, such as a shift of weight in the saddle or a slight twist of her hips. The horse responded immediately. He was doing well in walk, trot, and canter at the ask.

Nadine had left the trot poles in place at the far side of the ring. Today was his introduction. Some horses had strong reactions to anything new or unexpected, an abused horse even more so. One horse she had worked with would not walk over painted white lines on the ground.

But today, Stable Ticket showed his ability to trust and predict his rider. He walked over the poles, which were spaced evenly apart, to match his stride. He then trotted over them nicely as well. She ended the lesson with a walk around the outer edge of the ring.

Nadine carried the lunge line, halter, and lead rope as Dawn led the racehorse back to the barn by the reins.

"He's getting better, isn't he?" asked Dawn as the horse nudged her shoulder. He was eager for his treat.

"Yes and so are you," responded Nadine. "You are getting stronger lifting those saddles and hay bales. You are getting good at cleaning the stalls and turning out the horses."

As they entered the barn, Nadine saw lights flashing on the alarm system panel. There was a similar panel in the farmhouse that chirped audibly when any of the perimeters had been breached or when the cameras sensed movement by the gate. The barn panel only flashed. The entire farm property was encircled by perimeter guards about three inches off the ground. This easily detected any animal predators that may have crossed over them to threaten the horses.

The first driveway perimeter guard was three quarters of a mile away by the entrance on the main road. Nadine disliked surprise visitors. It had been breached while they were in the riding ring. She held up her hand to stop Dawn from getting Stable Ticket ready for brushing out.

Nadine clicked the driveway view camera. About twenty feet away from the closed electric powered gate was a black SUV. The driver could not be seen. Another perimeter alarm was ten feet from the gate. He had not tripped that one yet. She saw movement.

From behind the SUV, a man dressed in black clothes, tactical gear and wearing a balaclava covering his face stepped into view. He carried a sniper rifle with a telescopic sight.

Nadine spun around. "Put on your riding helmet," she urged Dawn, "we do not have much time." She took the reins from the child and repositioned the stirrups for a shorter rider. She led the racehorse out the back entrance of the barn by the bathing pad. "Hurry," she said as Dawn came out.

"You are going to ride for help," she said as calmly as she could. She boosted Dawn into the saddle and helped get her boots in the stirrups. "Heels, down," she reminded. "He's big, but he will listen to you. Follow the trail at the end of the paddocks. The one that leads to the ponds."

Dawn nodded, her newfound voice now silent as she realized what was happening.

"When you get to the fork, where it goes left to the ponds, go right. No need to run, a walk or trot will do. He has a bigger stride than Rampage, so make sure you hold the reins tight against his neck. He loves the trot but lean back so he will go down to the walk."

Nadine looked up at the frightened girl.

"You are light, like a jockey, so if you lean forward, he will think about racing. As scary as it might feel, sit up straight, hold your seat and let your legs be as long as you can. Imagine in your mind you can wrap them around his belly."

"In your mind, become part of the horse just like your serpentines on Willow," she continued. "Use your body to speak to him."

Dawn nodded, looking a little more collected.

"When you get to the end of the right-hand trail, you will come to a dirt road. Sugarcamp. Ride left on the road and it will lead into the village. This is all tribal land. The first farm on the right is Sam Red Deer's place. Ride right into the farmyard. Tell him we have intruders up here. I need help and the tribal police."

"Can you do that?" she asked.

Dawn nodded her head vigorously but did not speak.

"Stay with Red Deer's wife until an auntie comes for you. Do not leave the village. Do you understand?"

"Yes," a strained voice responded.

"Go now!" Nadine urged. "And Granddaughter, don't look back!"

The child rode away and did not look back.

He was easy to ride down the trail, like sitting on the top of a rolling couch. She felt breathless, her heart pounding, her mind racing. Slow down, she heard Nadine's voice in her mind. She thought, "my legs are wrapping around his belly."

The racehorse snorted.

She sat straight in the saddle and laid the reins gently on either side of his tautly muscled neck. Her whole body swayed, matching his walk. His ears pointed forward. He was listening.

One moment she felt she was simply on a trail ride, the next her heart pounded, thinking she would be caught and brought back to the kennel. Or worse. The man that shot Laney wanted to kill her, too.

The horse moved into a trot. She found her seat and posted. It had become second nature. It surprised her. The pace reassured her. She felt her heart beat to the rhythm of the racehorse's pace. One being.

He was strong. He would carry her to safety. They would get help for Nadine. She was safe.

As they turned onto Sugarcamp road, she leaned forward and lowered her head. Run, she thought. Do what you do best, she said in her mind.

He leaped forward and raced like the wind.

For the first time in her young life, she was fearless.

A Convergence of Crows

Nadine ran into the barn, closed the sliding doors, and lowered the inner bar. There was only one entrance to the barn now, the front. She had to close and bar it. Her rifle was in the farmhouse. It was too far to run across the open yard. She would be helpless against an armed, trained shooter with a sniper weapon. She rushed over to the alarm panel and clicked on the gate camera. The black vehicle was still there, but the shooter was not. It was a quarter of a mile from the gate to the stable yard.

He would probably go to the farmhouse first, thinking the girl was there. She had time. She went to the barn door, leaned out and began to close the heavy oak slider. The yard was utterly quiet; all the natural sounds of the forest had become silent. She had just enough time to realize what that meant when a bullet shattered the bones in her left arm.

The concussion of the high powered round threw her to the floor and her helmeted head hit the concrete floor. The horses began kicking the stall doors, snorting and neighing loudly.

Nadine spun over to her right side and leaped up. Blood poured from her wounded arm. She ran to the hayloft steps in the back of the barn and grabbed her Henry Big Boy rifle from its rack on the wall. The sniper's rifle had an eight hundred yard range; her weapon was only accurate to a hundred and fifty yards. It would have to do.

Adrenaline kicked in as she raced up the staircase. She grabbed white foreleg wraps from the tack box at the top of the steps and wound the strips tightly around her left arm. She twisted the leg wraps around her arm and used her teeth to knot it, nearly fainting from the pain of broken bones and ripped muscles.

She reached into the ammo box and stuffed 44 magnum caliber shells into her riding pants. The Henry was a lever action, center fire rifle that had deadly accuracy and could bring down big game. She armed it using her good hand to maneuver the Henry's side gate loader and chambered one of the powerful rounds.

Nadine quietly walked near the open hayloft door and stood carefully beside it. On either side were small loft windows with iron bars. She peered between the bars and was able to get a clear view of the farmhouse and the open yard. There was no one in sight. He had probably taken his shot from the woods behind the house.

The fading afternoon light cast the hayloft in shadows. She could not be seen. He would have to advance to the front of the barn. The back was barred and the stall windows were too small for human entry. He would have to come into range. She needed at least a hundred yards for a clear shot. But she would let him get much closer than that.

She had taken down a raging bull elk with the Henry, at twenty yards. She wasn't used to missing. She had staunched the bleeding, but her left arm hung uselessly at her side. She realized she could not use it to hold the gun.

Allowing her eyes to grow soft, her peripheral focus sharpened. This is how she hunted in the forest. Not all creatures made a noise. But they all moved. She exhaled and the searing pain moved to the edges of her mind. She listened. Not a sound. Not a twig snapped and yet she could feel him moving closer.

Whatever the child knew was enough to take down someone very powerful. That person had the resources to hire not one, but two hit men. The man who stalked her now was a highly trained killer. He had a heart of ice. She was a highly skilled hunter. She had ancestral rage. She never missed her target. She doubted he ever missed his. She would have to kill him with the first round and a one armed shot.

She listened. She waited. She watched. Her rifle could hold ten rounds, but only needed one to hit its mark. She was ready. She was silent.

She remembered when her daughter went missing. Her beautiful child had been eighteen; full of life and dreams. She remembered her daughter dancing in Grand Entry at the Powwows, her braids flying in rhythm. She saw the beautiful fringed shawl of rainbow woven colors proudly draped over her daughter's arm.

Missing. Raped and murdered by a white man.

It had occurred off tribal lands. No justice was possible. She had buried her only child ten years ago. She thought she had buried her own heart that day.

She thought of the day Dawn was brought to her by Spirit. A child that needed mending and her own broken heart that needed to be healed.

What is a cold murderer's heart compared to that of a mother whose heart beat with love and pounded with rage? No match, she thought as adrenaline coursed through her body.

Her keen hunter's eyes saw movement by a tree. She exhaled. She moved her head from side to side, like her totem's skill at perception. Hawk eyes. Missing nothing. Surviving eons by seeing mice and voles move in the underbrush one hundred feet below. Swoop and strike, beak and claw. She was no longer a human being defending her property; she was a creature hunting its prey.

He came out into the darkening yard as the sunlight faded. Black-clad, he moved toward the barn door, his rifle poised and aimed. He, too, watched for movement.

He came closer. He was twenty yards from the barn in the middle of the stable courtyard.

She leaped into the opened hayloft door with the Henry braced against her right shoulder. She aimed at the only vulnerable place, the balaclava. She shot him in the face with a single shell. The kickback threw her back onto the loft floor and she dropped the Henry.

Holmes lay on the ground, his dying body twitching and convulsing. His weapon had been blown out of his arms by the blast that had taken his life. The reverberation of the rifle blast died away and was replaced by the screams of crows as they broke from a cover of branches and flew into the darkening sky.

Then there was mayhem. The horses in the barn kicked the stalls, reared, neighing in terror. Six armed men in three ATVs drove wildly around the side of the barn. They had ridden up the Sugarcamp road. Each driver paired with a passenger prepared to shoot upon arrival.

Sam Red Deer drove his ATV up to the dead man on the ground. "Nadine!" He looked at the barn.

The other ATVs contained armed tribal police. They jumped out. "We will take over from here. Open the gate for the medic. Sam! Find Nadine," shouted one of the tribal officers.

As Sam Red Deer's cousin pressed the gate release button on the alarm panel, all the perimeter guards stopped flashing. Sam raced up the hayloft steps and found Nadine lying unconscious in a pool of blood.

She was bleeding from her arm, so he knew she was still alive. Only a beating heart pumped blood. He took off his belt, wrapping it as a tourniquet, and stopped her from bleeding out.

Moments later, the tribal medical clinic SUV arrived and medics raced up the steps. As they secured her wound and settled her on the gurney, she opened her eyes.

Nadine looked up into Anita McNee's gentle face.

"She's safe. Our little deer is safe," Anita said. Then Nadine passed out.

The tribal police staked crime scene tape around the shooter's body. This had happened on tribal lands. It was tribal jurisdiction and tribal law. There would be no actions taken against Nadine Thunderchild for what had happened here today.

Sam's cousin agreed to stay over night and feed the horses. In the morning, Fox would come to manage the farm until Nadine was able to return.

Joe Sands, the tribal police chief, got out of his truck. He had just arrived on the scene by the front gate. After hearing what had taken place, he took Sam Red Deer aside.

"Looks like Nadine finally shot herself a cowboy."

Rook Takes King

Tonhauer rubbed the Saluki behind her ears. Little Minx was his favorite. She was the only white-coated dog in his kennel. The fur on her long-haired ears was a blend of white and champagne colored wisps. She was gentle, loyal and good-natured.

Minx walked calmly by his side as he entered the film studio out building. She sat expectantly waiting for a treat she knew he kept in the pockets of his Sherpa lined, black Carhartt jacket. He surveyed the production set and the costume area. The film crew would be arriving soon. They were a well-paid team of men experienced in filming pornography and moonlighted on his special projects.

Tonhauer's film productions were an exceptional blend that catered to a very particular, high end audience that valued his exclusive content. They were also willing to pay a quarter of a million dollars per film, a unique performance for a single viewer. He sold the film performances to the highest bidder. One of a kind, as it were.

Often, the buyer had purchased one of the performers for a service in the past and now had the opportunity of watching her retirement performance of a lifetime. In the trade, it was referred to as 'snuff.'

The auction was announced in a brochure that arrived in his customers' email accounts. The name of the upcoming performer was listed as a show Saluki that was being retired. That would result in an immediate bidding frenzy among his select group of aficionados.

Most of his regular customers were celebrities, wealthy businessmen, foreign dignitaries and political players who enjoyed the anonymity of his "six-star" hotel services. He even counted a judge or two on his list of those who had a preference for a private, in person performance with a star of their choice.

The cadre of men who enjoyed his more elite services were frequent fliers to the island destination of Le Petite Beau Jardin. Reservations were by invitation only. The power of marketing surveys compiled with code language that revealed the profile of a particular psychological deviance enabled his private booking team to identify the kind of guests they were seeking.

Indigo Star was aging out of the six-star service circuit. She was an Indonesian beauty whose tawny skin and exotic gray-green eyes were highly popular with his more discerning customers. She would be missed for sure. But his talent team toured the world, finding suitable replacements, so the service industry he offered was easily replenish-able. There was always a family somewhere, so poor, so needy; they would sell a daughter to his team.

Indigo Star had come to the kennel when she was ten years old and had proven right away to be a priceless gem. But now she was twenty years old. The bidding on her final performance had begun in advance. A well-known investment banker with a penchant for peculiar sexual practices had won the bidding with a million dollar prepaid offer. He was obsessed with Indigo. When he learned of her retirement, he asked to buy her outright, but Tonhauer had refused. There was always the possibility that a girl would identify him or his team.

Indigo's final performance was worth more to him than any procurement opportunity she might have been coerced into providing. The recent defection of Fast Lane had alerted him that career advancement didn't always breed loyalty. Taking Ruby Tuesday with her was the final blow. He was pissed she used her freedom to bolt.

If Holmes had done his job right, both of those bad investments were extinguished by now. Indigo Star was up next. The prep area was ready, and the costuming had been laid out. The Rohypnol was on the dressing table by a glass of champagne, along with the makeup kit. Indigo Star was also the name of a glistening, dark blue opalescent nail and lip color. By this afternoon, it would be listed as no longer available.

The set design was ready and all the necessary props were laid out, including an eight-inch Damascus steel knife with a razor-sharp blade. As in past performances, he would be on set. He had a front row seat to a show that a narrow percentage of men found sexually exciting. Holmes' security team was scheduled for the perimeter patrol of the kennel grounds. All the kennel employees were off duty.

He tossed Little Minx her treat.

Helberg, Finch and the state police swat team were in position by the fire road. The advance team was in place, hidden in the woods by the front entrance to the kennels. Two troopers carried bolt cutters to open the back fence when given the order.

As the senior member of the team, Finch was the leader. But he relied on Helberg's special brand of operational strategy. She had scoped out the area the night before, creeping through the woods with a thermal reflex, night vision scope mounted on her rifle.

Using a combination of Google Earth and her skills in reconnaissance, she had drawn a complete map of the kennel grounds and out buildings.

The advance team radioed there was activity on the road. Several vans were arriving at the kennel gates. Finch indicated they were to stay in place. Moments later, they reported, a five-man team of armed guards was assembling in the kennel parking lot. The vans began unloading what looked like a news team with large video cameras.

Finch glanced at Helberg, but she remained expressionless. He ordered the advance team to observe but not engage. From the rear, none of what was taking place could be seen. Only the back and sides of the out buildings were visible. He nodded to Helberg.

They waited.

A tall man wearing a black jacket emerged from one of the buildings and signaled the crew of camera operators. They entered the building as he conversed with one of the armed men.

"Tonhauer," Finch identified the man to his team.

The armed security guards spread out and the advance team leader noted their positions to Finch. He confirmed three of the five guards patrolled the front gate area, which remained open.

The remaining two security guards were at that moment walking to the out building nearest to the back of the property. Tonhauer went into the kennels. Finch held up his hand and signaled the bolt cutting team to get ready.

Preparing a girl for her final performance was a particularly enjoyable moment for Tonhauer, as he found great pleasure in bestowing a retirement. He unlocked the gate on Indigo's cage. He took her by the arm and guided her toward the door. He grasped her elbow tightly, and she winced. He remembered another time he had guided her this decisively. It had been a private party in Manhattan attended by wealthy stock brokers and financiers. It was her introduction to a different class of sexual players. Indigo excelled beyond his expectations. Her exotic beauty generated an instant reaction in the crowded room. Every man wanted to possess her.

A girl's appeal as a child sexual performer for pedophile clients lasted until about age 15. After that, Tonhauer selected those young women whose features and skills could be groomed as both eye candy and privately procured escorts. He personally directed their specialized training.

Before the party, he had attended a fashion show with Indigo by his side. She was fascinated by the way the run-way models luxuriously demonstrated the fashion designs they wore. She would have been a natural for that industry, he had thought at the time, if she had had a different life. Indigo Star was one of those rare women who was as strikingly beautiful in an evening gown as she was stark naked.

He taught her the art of moving through a room without engaging eye contact with any of the men who stared at her. Her elegant demeanor immediately cast a spell of desire and she had been taught to act completely unaware of it. It was this aloof appeal he wished to recreate in her final film.

"This is your command performance," he said seductively. "After this, I'm letting you retire. And you know I treat my top stars generously. I am depositing two hundred million dollars in a Swiss account in your name only. You can create whatever life you want."

Her face registered shock, then wariness. She hesitated, smiled, and he gripped her elbow even more tightly. He smiled but his eyes were cold.

"Of course you will sign a contract that forbids you to mention my name, my organizations, the identities of my clients or any of the business you have conducted for me. The bank account serves as payment for any and all services you have performed. A small price for your freedom and an exorbitant gift of independence, don't you agree?"

She nodded.

"I have a script you will enjoy," he continued. "You play a run way model in this film. I have a number of designer outfits you can choose from. The scene includes a lascivious dinner with a stranger who finds you captivating. He will guide you in the performance, so follow his directions implicitly. As in other films, this one includes some bondage and a little violence, but nothing you can't handle."

She nodded nervously and smiled up at him. He guided her out into the kennel yard. He took as much pleasure in the cruelty of his lies as in the panicked realization she would experience right before her throat was cut in the final scene.

Helberg watched the pair through her binoculars and noted the young woman's long dark hair floating in the light breeze. As her attention captured every detail, her body registered sensations she could not explain. She felt a nearly overwhelming urge to protect the young woman, to extricate her from the tableau that was about to commence. She had seen collateral damage before, intimately. It would be easy for the young woman to get shot in the crossfire.

Trace felt inexplicably captivated by her delicate cheekbones and soft expression. As the state police team waited for Finch's advance signal, she plotted her opponent's possible moves, five steps ahead. There were many players on this board, Pawns and Knights, a Bishop or two. There was one King, one Queen and one Rook, herself.

If the op unraveled, the King would retreat to the back of the board, shielding himself with the Queen and relying on the two Knights in the back to take out the opposition. She looked at the fence line and her gaze landed on a receptacle for animal waste. She looked at the fence behind it and saw a gate. It was twenty-five feet away from the hidden swat team, Finch and herself.

Tonhauer would use the young woman for a shield and head in the direction of the gate. "I need to cover the alternative approach," she whispered to Finch. He nodded. She moved back toward the fire road, so silently and so imperceptibly he was convinced she was a ghost.

She positioned herself off the fire road behind a large tree. She held her rifle in a firing position. She was on the same path and

at the exact spot Johanna had stood when she turned off her
headlamp earlier that week.

Tonhauer and the woman entered the out building. Finch
gave the signal and the advance team burst on the scene. The
three armed guards fired their weapons and the swat team
engaged. The bolt cutters cut through the fence like butter.
Finch and the back team surged through the hole and headed
for the out building.

Cameramen ran out of the building and were quickly herded
by the advance team into custody. As swat officers swept into
the front door of the out building, Tonhauer emerged from
another door in the back, pushing the captive woman in front
of him. Two security guards flanked him on either side.

Sunlight glinted off the knife Tonhauer held at her throat.
Finch immediately told his team not to approach the tight four
person grouping.

"Hostage," he stated into the comm mike.

They were moving toward the back gate, with one guard
advancing ahead. Tonhauer and the girl faced the kennel
yard and walked backwards with the remaining security guard
between them and Finch's team. All guns were leveled at the
group as they moved toward the back of the property.

On the path now, they moved toward Helberg's solitary
position. Finch's team fanned out toward the cut in the fence,
as the guards, Tonhauer and his captive headed toward the fire
road.

Twenty yards away, Helberg stepped out onto the path, her rifle raised and scope aimed at the first security guard. She did not hesitate. She dropped him with a single kill shot to the head.

A swat officer shot the other guard and Tonhauer spun around to face Helberg, his knife pressed to Indigo Star's throat drawing a thin stream of blood. His left hand gripped her arm, and he pushed the woman forward roughly.

Trace knew he wouldn't kill his asset this early in the game. He was motivated to keep her alive as he had no more Pawns to spare.

Queen to Rook, 5, she thought.

The Rook moved back a space slowly. She focused on his face through her rifle scope. From years of watching the briefest flickers of expression across chessboards, she knew the fine distinction between a champion's determination and a competitor's misplaced confidence.

The King moved forward with the Queen between them.

Queen to Rook, 4. The Rook moved back another space. She saw the corner of his lip twitch, then draw up into the sliver of a vile grin. His cold eyes sparkled with contempt.

The King moved forward, his face now showing an arrogance born of unconscionable brutality. He forced her forward. The knife blade wavered loosely, inches in front of the woman's throat. The hilt, and the unsteady hand holding it, were now positioned in front of his chest.

Queen to Rook, 3. The Rook stepped back. She steadied the crosshairs of her sights on the King and his human shield. He had the empty soul of a man who ordered deaths the way other men ordered a pastrami sandwich. She was a highly trained killer who knew the precise moment in which a twisted belief in his own unbridled power fully distracted him. She knew a mind shaped by that kind of evil could not perceive defeat. His focus was consumed entirely on conquest.

She had a clear shot but could not take it. *If I shoot him in the head*, she thought, *he will fall back and cut her throat.*

It was as if he could read her thoughts.

The King's face registered triumph, believing he could play this right to the end and the trooper would not take a chance of accidentally shooting the hostage. He held Indigo Star even more tightly and moved forward. She paired her expert ability to instantly calculate every possible outcome of a tableau with her innate willingness to automatically take the advantage.

Queen to Rook, 2. The Valkyrie shot.

The full metal jacketed round pierced the hand holding the knife, shattering bone, vaporizing nerves and tendons as it passed into the King's heart, killing him instantly. Tonhauer dropped to the ground at the same moment the knife fell from his ruined hand. The woman screamed and collapsed onto the path, her arm reaching up.

"Don't shoot, please, don't shoot," she pleaded.

Trace lowered her weapon and reached down. She helped the young woman up and held her protectively around the shoulders.

'Please, there are more of us in the kennel. Help them please, please," she gasped.

Trace looked into the young woman's captivating gray eyes. "That's what we are here to do," she said softly.

A Daughter of the Moon and the Sun

Angelique reached for a cup of steaming coffee to start her day as sunlight streamed into Thunder Farm's kitchen. She opened the windows and breathed in the fresh, cool early morning air. It had been over two weeks since the attack on the farm. Nadine was now recovering from reconstructive surgery at the hospital, with weeks of painful physical therapy ahead of her. From her bed in intensive care, she hired Fox to manage the stables and work the horses with Dawn.

Angelique moved into the farmhouse temporarily. She wasn't alone. The tribal police had stationed a few men by the Sugarcamp road trail and by the main road leading to Nadine's farm. The alarm system was armed. Now that the traffickers knew the child's location, they needed to decide whether or not to move her.

One of the men from the community was a veteran who had seen active service in the military. He patrolled the surrounding woods, camping overnight. He was so well camouflaged; Angelique had not been able to detect his presence.

She had discussed Dawn's reaction to the traumatic events with Johanna the previous evening. The girl was more concerned about Nadine's injuries than the fact she herself had been the real target. As long as she knew Nadine was safe, she could focus on the horses. Nighttime was the hardest.

"This isn't over yet," Johanna had urged. "Let's find another safe place."

Angelique disagreed. "Tribal lands. Tribal law," she had stated. "We do not trust the United States' law enforcement to protect a mixed-race child or any child for that matter. They can't learn about her role in this nightmare. The tribal police have jurisdiction here and they will use it."

"These men have a lot to lose and they have deep pockets. Their security men are hired assassins."

"Our people are also ex-military. Remember, we have fought in every war the United States has ever engaged in. We, too, have the kind of lethal skills they have."

"How are they handling the dead guy?"

"They do not think his employers will be looking for him. He was not carrying any form of ID. Some shell company had a lease on the vehicle. No paperwork. Now *he* is a John Doe lying on a slab in a city morgue."

"There is some justice in that," responded Johanna. "Should I update Marti and Jayne about the attack?"

"No harm in doing that," Angelique had responded.

Fox would be arriving any minute to help with the horses. Dawn was in the barn feeding the horses bran mash before turning them out. After she and Fox cleaned the stalls, they would come to the farmhouse for breakfast.

Her cell phone buzzed, and she saw the text from Fox at the gate. She pressed the gate release button on the security panel and watched him drive in through the camera before locking the access again. They were on high alert.

Fox parked his truck by the barn and began loading hay bales onto the electric cart. He would toss a few flakes into each paddock while Dawn brought down the horses for the day. He was hoping to work with Merlin after breakfast. Loaded up, he drove the cart down the path to the lower field and paddocks.

Dawn attached lead ropes to Willow's and Rampage's halters and brought them down from the barn first. She took her time, walking slowly and confidently. She held a lead rope firmly in each hand and guided the big creatures down the path. Powerfully built, fast and strong, they followed her docilely.

She would bring Stormcatcher and Aquineh to their paddock next, and then Merlin by himself. Nadine had explained that Stable Ticket still had a track mind. He competed against other horses all his life. He won by running faster than any other horse that came near him.

"He is still unpredictable next to another horse. If he takes it into his mind to run, you can't stop him. Don't try. Drop his lead rope as soon as his shoulder muscles tighten. And always bring him down to the paddocks on his own."

Nadine had handled Stable Ticket with few exceptions. But the relationship between Stable Ticket and Dawn was unique. He was drawn to her in a way that was inexplicable. She had overheard Nadine tell Angelique they had a special bond.

She wasn't sure how to explain it, but Dawn could feel him in her mind. Twenty minutes later, all the horses were turned out, and she was rolling the wheelbarrow to the first stall with a pitchfork balanced over it. Fox joined her and cleaned the stalls on the other side of the barn.

He watched her deftly flip the clumps of manure into the barrow after sifting through the straw. "Hey, you're pretty expert with that pitchfork," he said.

She smiled and looked at him directly. She no longer felt apprehensive around him. He was tall as a man, but different from the men who had abused her. He was kind. She could feel it.

"I was thinking of working Merlin after breakfast, but maybe you can have a lesson on Stable Ticket instead. "

She walked over to Fox and looked up at him. Her dark eyes sparkled in her beautiful brown face. Her long black curls were caught up in a red bandana. "What's that?" she pointed to the tattoo on his forearm.

"A tattoo of a fox," he replied.

They finished their barn chores and headed to the kitchen to join Angelique for breakfast. Washing up first, Dawn removed the bandana and changed out of her work shirt.

"I just heard Nadine is coming home today," announced Angelique. "Your father is going to go get her, Fox. They should be here by mid-day."

After they finished eating, Fox walked down to the paddocks to bring up Stable Ticket while Dawn changed into riding clothes.

"Can I get a tattoo like Fox, Auntie? "

"What would you get?" she asked.

"I was thinking I could get the number that is on Stable Ticket's lip tattooed on my wrist. We are both rescues. That way, he won't belong to his owner anymore. He will be free like I am."

Angelique's breath caught in her throat.

"Thank you Auntie, for saving me that day."

Angelique took the girl in her arms and hugged her. "I will talk to your Grandmother about it," she promised.

She watched as the girl walked to the barn. Our little deer is healing beyond anything we could have imagined, she thought.

An hour later, Fox lunged the black racehorse in the riding ring as Dawn watched from the fence. Fox had a plan.

Angelique watched from the porch as he boosted Dawn onto the horse's bare back. She watched the girl lengthen her legs around the horse's belly. She gathered the lower part of his mane in her hands and nodded to Fox. No reins, no saddle, just a lunge line. Fox began to walk the racehorse around the ring's outer perimeter. The rider moved in perfect alignment with the horse's rhythm at a slow walk.

Fox walked beside them, holding the line. "The bottom of your spine is directly on his. He will feel your muscles clench. If you are unsure, he will see what he can get away with. If you are confident, he will listen and follow your lead."

Dawn felt the connection come together, the base of her spine against the hard spine of the horse. They moved together. There was no separation between them, no stirrups to lean into or balance her, no reins to give directions. She could feel the ripple of his rib muscles flex under her thighs. It was just her mind and his mind; just her body and his.

"Now close your eyes," Fox said. "Feel more than see. Feel the texture of his mane in your hands, feel the way your body moves with his, one fluid motion. Relax your shoulders, relax your legs. Take in a deep breath and let it out slowly.

"Let's take it up." Fox started to jog, and the horse began to trot. Around the ring once, twice and then Fox called out, "let go of his mane and put your arms out to the sides, up in the air. Find your balance with your eyes closed."

Angelique watched as Dawn raised her arms lateral to her body and Fox reached up and unclipped the lunge line. He stepped back to the center of the ring, holding the rope.

She rode the powerful black horse into a canter, her arms outstretched, eyes closed.

They are flying, Angelique thought.

Dawn felt the moment they became one mind, her breath coming in spurts matching his breath as he pounded the earth. She felt his next movement as if it were her own. She lowered her arms and grasped his mane. Slow down, she thought. He came down to the walk. Stand still, she thought as she straightened her shoulders back. He slowed and stopped. She opened her eyes and gasped.

She had thought Fox had been running alongside them the whole time. He now walked toward them from the center of the ring with the lunge line dangling from his hand.

"It was like riding the wind," she said. She dismounted and landed strongly on her feet in the soft dirt.

He smiled and nodded. "Nothing like it, is there? His mane was flying and his tail straight out. "

"That's who he is, Fox," she said excitedly. "He's the Wind."

"His true name," responded Fox. He handed her the lead rope as he rolled up the lunge line. "All yours. A horse like that will only share his mind with one rider."

As Angelique watched, the pair walk the black racehorse down to the paddock, her cell phone buzzed. It was Nadine. She remotely opened the gate to let Sam's truck enter.

Nadine and Angelique sat on the porch after lunch, the taller woman's left arm in a sling. Sam Red Deer had left. Dawn and Fox were down at the paddocks. Anita had called to say she was coming by to check on her patient.

It was late afternoon when she finally arrived. She handed Nadine a plastic bag containing Josette's hairbrush. She held up a report from the lab.

"It is official," she said to the other women. "According to this DNA analysis, Dawn is Josette's daughter."

"What?" Nadine reacted. "That is impossible."

"Of course it's impossible," said Anita. "But the lab report is accurate. There were enough follicles on the remaining hair strands in Josette's hair brush to extract DNA that closely matched the DNA on the saliva sample I took from you, Nadine, across 3,477 centimorgans. The percentage of that being a parent-child relationship is 100%."

"Of course it is," said Angelique. "Josette is Nadine's daughter, and it was her hair sample."

"Well, I submitted the samples under slightly different names," said Anita. "See?" She held up the report.

The report identified the saliva sample as obtained from Josette Pretty Dove Lawson. It listed the DNA from the hair follicles as being collected from Dawn's "Jane Doe" rape exam when it was actually switched from samples removed from Josette's hairbrush. The switched results indicated that Jane Doe was Josette's daughter.

"Labs do not lie. The only thing wrong were the labels on the test kits," said Anita. "Our little deer is truly your granddaughter now. By the way, I used all the hair samples on Josette's hair brush. Now there are no longer any remaining gene samples to refute these results."

"A granddaughter by Spirit is as good as full blood," laughed Angelique.

"Dawn is the daughter of the moon and the sun," said Nadine. "Who are we to argue?"

Back to Back

Johanna sat on the ground in the middle of one of the gardens. She dug her bare toes into the warm soil and looked up at the sky. The heat of the sun on growing gourds filled the air with the unmistakable scent of pumpkin. She closed her eyes and let her ears drink in the sounds of crickets and bees, chickadees and the wild scree of a circling eagle. She felt complete. The sound of footsteps came from the far side of the garden.

Scott approached slowly, not wanting to disturb her. "There's a rainstorm coming," he said softly. "Can you smell it?"

She opened her eyes and nodded.

"You looked like you were dreaming," he said.

"I was thinking of canning pumpkin puree so I could bake fresh pumpkin muffins this coming winter."

He looked around the patch at the multitude of pumpkins with their thick, twisted, woody vines. "That's a lot of muffins."

She laughed. "I will only need a few pumpkins. The rest can go to the Coop market for sale."

"Maybe we could donate them to the childcare center for Halloween projects instead," Scott asked.

"That's a much better idea."

He sat down in the dirt next to her, back to back. She tilted her head against the hollow of his shoulder and looked up again at the sky. She could feel the bones in his spine against her own. She could feel his body move as he breathed.

"A package came for you today at the post office," he said. "I left it on the table. It's from Minerva's Meadows Herb and Tea Garden in Maine."

"That must be from Norah. She said she would send me her new herbal tea blend to try. She said lavender and rose are very soothing."

"Would she help design your medicinal herb garden?"

"Yes, I have a good start on the garden plan, but Norah is an expert," Johanna said.

They lapsed into a comfortable silence. The sound of crickets and the wind blowing through the branches of the trees was a comforting backdrop for their private thoughts. Their bodies braced against one another.

Johanna felt a sudden sadness welling up within her heart. She remembered how hard it was for her when she and Scott divorced. She did not know how she could bear losing Scott again. This time for good, she thought. We all die and lose one another. It will happen some day. It's inevitable. She felt the hard strength of his back against her own.

The visceral presence of his body was like the vital assurance of earth, sky, wind and rain. His body reminded her that she was alive, his touch made her body respond with a depth of joy and connection it could not provide on its own. She sighed.

Scott rested, feeling the warmth of Johanna's body. She was a constant in his life. He did not want a single day to pass without her presence. He loved her deeply, as he always had, even when they argued and separated. He felt his life come apart when they divorced. He'd believed he was a failure. Right now, by her side, he felt at peace within himself.

This newly crafted togetherness was a double-edged sword for him. She had a place in his life again. He wanted to give her everything. He wanted to make her happy. He wanted to see her smile. He knew her clinical practice had been tearing her apart, even though she, herself, could not see the enormous cost at the time. The solar farm was giving her back the peace and joy he felt she deserved. I could not bear to lose her again, he thought. And yet, one day, one of us must leave the other.

A raindrop splashed on Johanna's face, another on the ground beside her.

"It's raining," Scott said.

"I can feel it," laughed Johanna, "a warm summer rain."

They sat together as the skies opened up and rain poured down on the thirsty land. Their clothes were soaked and still they sat like two children in the rainstorm.

"I have an idea," said Scott. "Let's go to the outdoor bath and take a shower in the rain together."

Johanna smiled and stood up. Her rain soaked shirt revealed soft curves. When she was a younger woman, those same muscles were taut from years of yoga. Scott was no less attracted to the softness of her aging, as the years had been gentle with her. Lovemaking was not reserved for the young, he thought, and that was the best kept secret of all.

Moments later, they left their muddy garden sandals by the concrete patio shower blocks. They stood together naked under a stream of fresh artesian well water and warm summer rain. They soaped one another's body, touching places on one another that were as familiar to them as their own skin.

"There's something I need to tell you," she said, looking deeply into his eyes. She thought it would be best to tell him about her dangerous adventure with Angelique.

"Later," he said as he touched her lips with his fingers and the warm rain rinsed their bodies.

Toweling off, they went into the cabin to spend the rest of the stormy afternoon in bed, beneath the skylight. The gentle sound of newly installed copper rain bells ringing in the Buddha garden filled the room. They moved together wordlessly, making love and then slept in one another's arms. A synergy of Yin and Yang each contained within the opposite. Their bodies were like one body.

The Truth About Fast Lane

J ayne leaned into Marti's study. "Movie night?"

"Sounds great. Let me put this stuff away and we'll look over our options." Marti began to clear her desk. The phone rang, and she instinctively reached for the landline console. Jayne rolled her eyes.

"Burke Security Agency, Marti O'Neil speaking."

"O'Neil? It's Trace Helberg. We need to talk."

The next morning, Marti waited for Helberg in a local coffee shop. She felt nervous. Apparently, the investigator had questions. She tightened her shoulders and prepared herself.

A tall, wide shouldered young woman with spiked red hair and piercing blue eyes entered the cafe. She wore black pants with a black sweater. She pushed a pair of Oakley sunglasses up behind her ears like a hairband. Her stance and command gave her away. This woman wouldn't last undercover for a minute,

Marti thought; she has no idea how to blend. She raised her
hand, signaling the booth in the back where she was sitting.

Marti stood up to introduce herself. She was surprised at the
woman's height and the strength of her handclasp. They sat
down on either side of the booth as the state trooper ordered
a cup of coffee.

"I need to know if the witness who contacted you ever called
back," Trace asked.

"No," responded Marti. "If she had, I would let Finch know
immediately."

"Fair enough."

"I don't know what I can add," said Marti preemptively.
"Finch was thorough."

"What your witness saw and shared enabled us to take down
a child-sex trafficking ring."

Marti met Trace's gaze full on and directly. "So it wasn't just
a drive-by shooting?"

"That photo enabled us to tie together two of the traffickers'
deaths and your witness's statement helped identify key
evidence in the female victim's possessions that broke the
trafficking operation wide open."

"What was that?"

"I can tell you because that part of the investigation is over,
but it's not going to make the news. There was a small flash
drive hidden in a tube of lipstick on the floor of the woman's
car. It contained copies of sex videos involving a child and a
well-known senator, a sex performance video of the Camry

driver, and a snuff film in which a young Hispanic woman was brutally raped and murdered."

Marti's throat suddenly went dry, and her heart raced as if she were running a marathon. Trace watched her face carefully and noted the momentary look of shock.

"We discovered a dog kennel in a small central Pennsylvania town where they kept the girls. A hotel chain businessman who was fronting the trafficking ring owned it. We were able to bust the operation and rescue eight girls ranging in age from twelve to twenty years old."

Marti nodded, trying to regain her composure.

"The head of this organization was shot and killed while trying to escape with a hostage. We are still investigating key members of his operation as well as some high-profile clients who took part in illegal activities."

"One of the trafficked girls told us about Elaine Webster, who was the shooting victim at the Ice Mine Cut. She was a sex trafficking victim herself who had become a procurer for the ring," Trace continued. "She apparently downloaded incriminating evidence onto the flash drive before disappearing from the property. It isn't clear if she was planning to blackmail the politician involved or just needed evidence to trade for her freedom."

"It got her killed," Marti stated bluntly.

"That it did," responded Trace. "One more thing, though. The girl told us that Webster, also known as Fast Lane, took more than a flash drive with her. She also took a child whose film name was Ruby Tuesday. We found two passports," Trace paused, "a woman's and a child's."

"Holy shit," said Marti.

"Right," said Trace, looking directly at Marti with a no nonsense steel blue gaze, "so where's the kid?"

Marti felt her heart simultaneously pound as her stomach sank. She kept her face as neutral as possible, using every element of undercover police training she had.

Trace waited a full minute before adding, "At first, I thought the passport was for the missing girl. But no, the name on the passport was Rosalita Martinez. The birth date indicated she would have been eighteen, currently. According to one of the girls, Rosalita was the girl in the snuff film."

Marti looked down at her hands. She was taking a gamble. She needed a moment to break Trace's gaze and to redirect her without appearing to do so. She sighed. Her shoulders relaxed. She looked up.

"So, where's the missing girl?" Marti asked.

"We don't know," responded Trace. "It's possible your witness, Marcia Davenport, took her from the scene. But we have no idea who that woman really is. We may never find the child at this point."

"Then it's unlikely Davenport will ever contact me again," said Marti.

"You know what to do if she does."

Trace finished her coffee and slid her contact card across the table toward the other woman. "If anything comes up."

Marti nodded, and Trace stood up.

After the trooper left the coffee shop, Marti decided it would be better to use Jayne's phone to contact Johanna.

In the early hours, right before dawn, a red truck came around the corner of the Ice Mine Cut and slowly drove onto the access road, coming to a stop. It was still dark. A fragrant moon illuminated both the road and the face of the cliff with pale, merciless light.

Angelique turned off the headlights, leaving the yellow fog lamps glowing. The passenger door opened. Anita's footsteps crunched on the gravel as she walked toward the place where the maroon Camry had come to rest a few months before.

The shadowed silence was broken only by the sound of the river rushing one hundred feet below and the wind rustling briskly through the trees. She walked over to a flat boulder beside a guardrail that blocked huge sliding cliff rocks from smashing onto the road below.

Anita stood in the space where another woman had lost her life. It was a place tainted by human hatred, betrayal, and death. This space between the towering cliffs and the river-bend needed a blessing. She waited patiently.

Behind her, a waxing gibbous moon tightly grasped the night as the rising sun before her held the new day in tendrils of glowing golden light. She stood in a fierce narrow cleft of black silken shadows. She was betwixt, between and within indelible arcs of elemental forces as ancient as the formation of the earth itself. Great forces were gathered at the precise moment day pierces the night.

Anita held a tobacco tie in her right hand. The tobacco was very old. Fifty years had passed since it had grown in the soil and she had gathered it in a sacred way. In her left hand, she held loose tobacco that was crumbling into dust.

She spoke words from an ancient language as she sprinkled the tobacco from her left hand onto the ground. These words were never to be translated into any form or sound other than those given to the people by the Creators. These were words that healed the energy in a space beyond any action a human could contrive.

Her gift was not an easy one. Unlike Johanna's gift, she did not just see the world through another person's eyes. She was abruptly shapeshifted into the body of that person, to vividly feel their last experience of life. She knew that the moment of death was a pivot upon which the earth's elemental forces were drawn with great love and respect.

The Medicine Woman placed the tobacco tie on the flat rock. It would tenderly carry the soul of the woman who had died there to the worlds of Spirit. In that moment, crows called to one another in the forest and the crisp, crystalline air coalesced into swirls of shadows and light.

She was filled with dread and her heartbeat rose in terror. She had guided the Camry away from the edge of the cliff road as the white truck tried to push them over the ledge into the river. She fought the wheel as the car spun on the road and came to rest on the access road to the cliffs.

He was getting out of the truck. She had only moments left. The cosmetic bag had spilled onto the passenger side floor. She grabbed the lipstick tube. No one knew what she had taken and hidden on the hard drive. It was to be their ticket out of hell and any others that information could save. She only had a moment to realize... I should have changed the license plate.

She turned to the girl in the back seat. "I am so sorry," she said. "I tried." Then her world exploded into light.

Anita saw it all, felt it all, as if it were happening to her. She bowed her head. The sunlight from the rising dawn formed a pool of warm light around her.

"You brought her this far, Laney," she said to the milky white vapor as it receded within the shadows, "we took her the rest of the way. She is safely home and so may you be, as well."

She turned to the moon as it faded into a pale white circle now on its journey to the other side of the world. "May all who are lost find their way safely home."

She blew the remnants of crumbled tobacco into the wind. She smelled the distinctive sweet scent of the dried, never-burned leaves on her fingers as her prayer floated up to the Wind Sisters and was borne away to the four directions.

She walked over to the truck and got in. Angelique put it in reverse, backed up and then put it into drive. She gunned the accelerator, and they drove back the way they had come.

Shadows and Light

*T*he sun set the sky on fire with purple and orange clouds
that whirled like flames. She made her way silently along
the mountain ridge, as her kind had perfected over many eons
of time. She trotted along a path lined with the starkly twisted
skeletal shadows of apple trees. Her face lifted as she caught the
sweet fragrance of fruit that blended with the acrid scent of
humans. She stopped to drink at the cool waters of the upper
pond that overlooked the dwelling below. Momentarily, she gazed
at her reflection in the mirrored water. It wavered within the
flaming mirage of clouds and sky. As above, so below, she thought.

She blinked her golden eyes, and the images dissolved and
reassembled. Of all the medicine teachers she had stalked, this
one was surprisingly unique. The woman had no pretentiousness
to unravel or desire to control others that she would have to
dismember before sharing her medicine knowledge. From mind
to mind, ancient wisdom transferred from teacher to student as
fluidly as the wind moved across the lands when their humanness
didn't interfere.

Crafting a shaman took a great deal of effort. In her experience,
the more skilled the student, the more difficult it was for them to

accept working with power. Which was just as well. She was adept at the art of dismembering those that sought to use this power to serve their own greed. But this woman with the long silver hair was different. She seemed to know the importance of being humble when working with elemental beings.

Her reflection shimmered and shifted in the shadowed waters. For the briefest of moments it revealed a swirl of softly feathered plumes bursting in a cacophony of bright colors and rainbow light. Fierce eyes of frozen starlight stared back at her, then vanished.

Oh, so many forms, thought the shape-shifter.

Dawn Rides the Wind

I t had been nearly a year since Johanna had discussed Marti's
phone call with Angelique, in which they learned the
outcome of the investigation. During the months that followed,
several of the kennel's employees had decided to cooperate with
the prosecution team. While Tonhauer himself would never
face a jury, key managers of his hotel and island operations
would. The Guardian Security firm was facing separate charges
of murder as well as human trafficking.

Abel Finch, the leading investigator, identified a politician,
a corporate executive, and a judge who appeared in the three
videos found on the hidden flash drive. Those findings had
opened the door to seizing the Little Mountain Saluki Kennel's
computer files which had been backed up on an offsite location.

Those company records revealed a number of high-profile
senators and business associates who had been Tonhauer's
customers and frequent visitors to the island locations. Their
purchases of Chaude au Coeur nail cosmetics coincided with
the retirement of the identically named Saluki dogs. While those
purchases did not constitute permissible evidence, the timelines

that coincided with the videos that identified those customers did.

At the time, Johanna was confident the videos the state police had found on the hard drive would be enough evidence to take down the entire Beau Jardin enterprise, including a location on a private island. The girls they had rescued at the kennel had agreed to testify.

"However," Johanna had revealed to her friend, "the state police know one of the girls is missing and assume the witness must have taken her. I can't quite envision their giving up a search for a missing girl."

Angelique had raised her eyebrows. "Well, I can. They do it all the time with mixed-race and native women. They honestly don't care. They will process the report, but they won't expend the manpower to find them. I will tell Nadine. Our little deer has a new home and Nadine has a granddaughter."

It was now mid October and the morning air was crisp. Johanna settled back in Angelique's truck for a long drive to one of Connecticut's local dressage shows. Dawn was competing at the introductory level for the first time, and Nadine had invited them to attend.

They found the equestrian center in Ellington, where the competition was being held. Angelique located the riding ring for the morning dressage events. Moments later, they walked to a corner of the field where Thunder Farm's horse trailer was parked. The sky was cerulean blue with white puffy clouds and the air was cool, a perfect day for a horse show.

The four women stood at the riding ring's fence line as Nadine pointed out the young rider mounted on the black thoroughbred by the entrance gate. Fox held Wind's bridle, steadying Dawn before her entry to the ring. There were four riders before her. She was the fifth and final entry in the Intro B dressage competition.

She wore tan breeches, a starched white shirt and a black competition jacket. Her curly black hair was pulled back with a black bow under her velvet helmet and she was smiling. She leaned forward and patted the horse on his finely muscled neck. Fox looked up at her and grinned.

"Is she nervous?" asked Johanna.

"Probably," responded Nadine, "but she has practiced this test for a month now. She is ready."

The announcer stated, "Dawn Lawton riding The Wind for Thunder Farms." Rider and horse entered the ring.

"Good," said Nadine. "Walking trot rising."

The horse approached the center line at a medium walk, halted at the center X point and the rider saluted the judges before beginning the dressage test.

"She is tracking left at C, again, working trot rising," said Nadine, her voice low and precise. She nodded as horse and rider fluidly entered the turn. "He is balanced and bending through the turn."

"At E, she circles left 20 meters, still in the working trot rising....."

Angelique, Anita, and Johanna watched the girl's contained but flexible posture and skill in giving barely noticeable signals to the horse. Wind did exactly as she asked.

"She is keeping the roundness and size of the circle accurate, he has a clear trot rhythm and bend," continued Nadine softly.

"Between K and A, she is developing a medium walk...the horse must be willing and balanced.... yes. The transition to walk rhythm was smooth and complete."

"From F to E, now is the free walk," Nadine continued to narrate the test. "There must be complete freedom for him to stretch his neck forward and downward. Wind has a clear walking rhythm on the diagonal with plenty of ground cover."

They watched Dawn gather the reins after passing the E point.

"A little late on that," said Nadine, "E to H must be a medium walk. He has to have willing and balanced transitions. Yes, good."

"From H to C, another working trot rising....."

"At B, she circles right for a 20 meter circle at the working trot rising.... Their circle is nicely rounded. It's not as easy as they are making it look," added Nadine. "They have been practicing circles for weeks. Clear trot rhythm and bend, nicely done...."

The other women could clearly see the perfect circle of hoof prints in the ring.

"At A, she is coming down the center line... straight through the center line. Wind is willing and balanced in a medium walk as they transition to the halt," Nadine said.

Dawn halted Wind by straightening her back and gave a slight, nearly imperceptible touch of the reins. Wind stopped and Dawn dropped her head for the salute.

"Well done," said Nadine. "A couple of errors, but it should not have cost her too many points."

Horse and rider then approached the judges for their final notes and were instructed to wait before the judging stand. The other riders returned to the ring and lined their horses up beside one another for the awarding of the ribbons. The competition steward attached a different colored ribbon to each of the horses' bridles, then the riders left the ring.

Fox assisted Dawn as she dismounted the tall thoroughbred. She led Wind to the trailer, where she and Fox unsaddled and put on his halter. There was a hay bag slung on a hook by the ramp so he could eat his fill. Dawn helped saddle Merlin for the jumping events, which were coming up next. Fox was riding him for Thunder Farms.

She approached the four women. She was tall for a twelve-year-old, as slender as a reed with her dark, tight curls spilling out of their velvet bow and net. She walked with her shoulders straight, a confident smile, and carried a red ribbon in her hands.

"For you, Grandmother," Dawn handed the award to Nadine.

"Second place." Nadine handed it back. "All yours, Granddaughter!"

Angelique smiled. Anita hugged the girl proudly.

Dawn looked up at Johanna's face. "I remember you," said softly. "You are one of the aunties."

"That's right," said Johanna.

"Thank you for coming to see me ride," she said.

Hearing the girl's soft voice for the first time and seeing the confidence and pride in how she held her body brought tears to Johanna's eyes. If she had been a trauma client of hers, Johanna would have therapeutically retraced the steps of healing for her. She would have acknowledged the powerful path from victim to survivor this child had traversed. But she was not Johanna's client and would never need to be.

"I wouldn't have missed it for world, Dawn," she responded, using the girl's name for the first time.

She was nearly as tall as Anita and would likely grow to be the height of Angelique or Nadine. She hugged Johanna tightly as the pungent smell of leather and horse drifted up between them. An image slowly began to weave together in Johanna's mind.

She saw Dawn dancing in a circle with other young girls. Their long black braids whipped through the air. She was wearing a yellow doeskin dress with soft boots and fringed leggings. She was carrying a sky blue shawl over her arm with symbols of lightning and wind embroidered in colorful beads and edged with black fringes.

A dance shawl, Angelique had once explained, was designed and made by a girl, each one of a thousand single fringes tied and knotted by hand. It was the connection between the Creators, that girl, and her ancestors. It was her lineage to Starwoman.

Dawn stepped back with a deep smile. She went to Anita and Angelique, hugging each in turn. Moments later, she walked away to hold Merlin while Fox changed into his breeches, shirt, and competition jacket in the trailer.

Dawn and Fox traded being handlers for the horses at the shows, so Nadine was free to talk to prospective buyers about her rescue retraining work with off track thoroughbreds. But today, Nadine explained, the horses were not for sale.

"Merlin is spoken for," she said. "Fox has nearly worked off the sale price. And Wind clearly belongs to Dawn."

"Does she know it yet?" asked Angelique.

Nadine shook her head. "Not yet. I want her to feel she earned him with her own work and efforts. Gifting is a natural way of life to our people," she explained to Johanna. "So is trade that is equitable and fair. I want her to know she has value. So her work is traded for her skill and responsibility. Overtime, she will earn Wind."

"You have a gift, Nadine," said Anita, "a true healing gift with horses and wild deer. This child is a different girl than the one I came to examine so long ago. Whatever happened to that other girl?"

"She went away," responded Nadine. "She left."

"That one is no more," said Angelique.

Johanna suddenly realized they were not talking metaphorically. They really meant the victim was gone. The young girl holding the reins of a powerful racehorse was not a survivor of abuse, with a lifelong path of healing ahead of her. She was a healed person who had left her suffering entirely behind her and had walked onto a new trail.

All western medicine offered was medication and a form of brutal mind surgery called psychotherapy. Therapists used man made theoretical tools with elaborate techniques as if those were, themselves, a treatment. Spirit offered no treatment at all. It merely provided an opportunity to walk on a completely new path.

She realized, then, the shaman stone she had tossed into the kennel yard wasn't just the means of interfering with a vile organization that profited from sexual slavery. It was a spiritual force of power that altered the course of evil and reshaped everyone involved.

The girl named Ruby Tuesday was gone forever and so were all the other girls with show dog names. They had been given new lives. She, herself, was altered as were Nadine, Anita and Angelique.

No one was the same person they had been before Spirit brought Angelique around the corner of the Ice Mine Cut at the precise moment a gunman was poised to kill a child. The shaman stone did so much more than help take down a sex trafficking ring.

As if she read her mind, Angelique suddenly asked Johanna to explain the shaman stone she used to Nadine and Anita. Johanna then recounted the story of how the river told her where to find the stone and how to ask for its help. She described how she painted it and drove to Little Mountain.

She explained what happened when she walked down the path that led to the kennel on a moonless night and tossed the stone over the fence. She described how her eyes had changed their focus and how she wanted to leap over the fence and attack the people who held the girls prisoner.

"It was so hard to know they were likely in those kennel buildings and to leave without setting them free," Johanna said sadly, her voice catching in her throat with tears.

"That is why you shape shifted into another creature," said Anita. "The human in you wanted to set them free. But Spirit had a bigger plan."

"You have a very powerful teacher," Angelique offered. "She came to me looking for a new student. I knew you were the right one."

"Mountain lion," answered Johanna. "She sure is a task master."

Angelique laughed. "Indeed she is. They all are. Your people think spirit animals are benevolent Disney cartoon creatures. They are anything but!"

"No disrespect," said Anita, grinning. "But we would like to keep it that way."

"I understand," nodded Johanna. "I have been learning a meaning of honor and respect that my culture has no concept of. This teacher has a plan for me that I probably can't even imagine."

"Try having a bat for a spirit teacher," said Angelique.

Nadine took Johanna's hands and looked softly into her eyes. "Spirit found a way to restore my daughter to me by giving me a granddaughter to love. Thank you for your part in that, Netuksq."

Johanna nodded, realizing Angelique had shared her name with the others.

"Johanna," said Angelique, "I have always honored the work you do with your trauma clients. You helped them find their voice, their strength, and a new purpose for their lives. You thought you were giving them the tools to fight their abusers and live their lives without fear. But you were really doing direct battle with their perpetrators all along."

Johanna looked confused.

Anita smiled gently; her bright eyes glittered in her darkly lined face. "See, when an abuser attacks someone, rapes them, murders them, they have stolen that person's innocence, their freedom, strength, sometimes even their very life. If the person survives the attack, they are left with shame, humiliation and fear."

Johanna nodded. She had seen the effects of this kind of brutal dis-empowerment throughout her career. A seventy-year-old woman she once worked with recounted an incident that happened when she was a young woman in which her home was broken into. She was raped, strangled and left for dead. She regained consciousness when sunlight finally came through her bedroom windows. She was unable to sleep in a room with the curtains drawn closed for the rest of her life. Paradoxically, open curtains meant she was safe, because she could see the sky.

"All these years," continued Anita, "you have been attacking abusers in a stealthy fashion, like a mountain lion. You have been stealing back the innocence, freedom, and self-esteem they took from their victims. You have been giving the abusers back the shame and fear that actually belong to them, alone. This is a powerful way to do battle. The foe never sees you defeat them."

Angelique smiled. "Your people keep thinking mountain lions are disappearing as predators because their numbers are down. You don't see them, so you think they are gone. But they are night stalkers. They are smart. They live in their own way on their own lands and stay away from those who would harm them. They take their prey when their own attackers are asleep. You never see them."

"As long as you believe they are vanquished, they will survive under your very noses," said Nadine.

"And we would like to keep it that way," responded Anita.

"Yes, that mountain lion is a good teacher," added Angelique.

"The jumps are up," Nadine pointed to the riding ring.

The four women stood along the fence line as Fox rode Merlin into the ring. Horse and rider trotted to the center line and saluted the judges.

Dawn walked toward the four women and took her place among the crows. Then there were five.

Epilogue

Scott came in the door with a handful of freshly plucked late season corn. Johanna stood by the kitchen sink looking out across the gardens of Elk Run farm.

"I saw mountain lion tracks in the field again," he said.

One Crow: "Pay Attention!"

The Medicine Woman entered her evidence room and removed the unlogged rape kit for a child named Jane Doe. Leaving the clinic, she drove to a ceremony in the forest attended by two tall women, each with long, flowing dark hair.

The burn pit glowed with hot, red embers. The taller of the two women added cedar to the coals and fanned the growing flames. The younger one added a tobacco tie. The Medicine Woman threw the box into the fire.

Three Crows: "They are talking about you."

Afterword

Some of these events are true; in fact they happen all too often. Most of the characters are fictitious. All of the wisdom is real. My stories are written using a traditional literary storyteller device called writing the braids. Each story is a braid woven together by three independent stories, or strands, that come together for a central theme. The central theme is like the ribbon that binds the braids together. The ribbon that binds A CONVERGENCE OF CROWS is 'honor.'

The first strand of the braid is the story of high-ranking privilege and the trafficking of human beings. The second strand is how US law protects crimes against indigenous people from being punished. The third strand is the story of Johanna's path of ancient shamanic training and her introduction to a worthy spirit teacher who tracks her relentlessly like prey.

The Shaman's Gift

I encourage you to get acquainted with Nature and her many ways of teaching wisdom. You do not need to be a Shaman, a Medicine Person, or have any special training to experience her gifts in all of their forms.

If you enjoy hiking, gardening, the majesty of her peaks and oceans, her lakes and ponds, her forests and creeks, you are already aware she is no ordinary inert object. She is alive and all her creatures, plants and vegetation have been gifted with the power of ancient knowledge. Embedded in their collective DNA is how to survive, thrive, propagate and share their unique gifts. Even rocks, mountains and soil have timeless wisdom.

Humans, it is clear, are deeply wounded beings who seek meaning and connection. We too have been gifted with ancient knowledge yet we do not know how to access it. We have become disenfranchised from our own wisdom seeds.

Many people seek this knowledge through mystical practices. They have been led to believe that something outside themselves holds the answers. This is a fundamental mistake. It's true, the answer is outside. Outside in Nature. It's our connection we have lost. It's our connection we must recover.

Here is a guided shamanic journey I recorded. It helps identify your embedded relationship to the Earth and all her elemental beings. Listen to this journey, then, afterwards, see how different the world appears to you.

~ Anneka

https://bit.ly/ShamansGift

Acknowledgements

Thank you Celeste Longacre for letting me learn in your gardens.

Thank you Ahanecqa for teaching me your mysterious ways.

Thank you Skye Jones for the off-track thoroughbred racehorse rescue and re-training work you do at Bayside Equestrian. Thank you for your excellent narration of an Intro B Dressage Test.

Thank you Kerrie Peters for law enforcement and forensic information.

Thank you Jess Kielman and Gayle Andrew for the late night plot jams, blueberry pie, and the sweetest of baklava.

I am deeply grateful to my Beta Readers who offered support, editing, suggestions, eagle eyes and so much more: Shari Lynch, Louise DeSantis Deutsch, Lisa Kearley Elder, Melanie Dawn Hogan and Claire Wagner Kimball.

With much gratitude, I would like to thank Erica Shay, author of the Tarot Mystery series who allowed her characters Marti O'Neil and Jayne Cullen to appear in this book.

Look for further involvement in future Johanna Kincaid shaman mysteries. Meanwhile, I recommend reading:
The Ace of Cups: Her First Time Out
By Erica Shay

Notes

*The Whiskey Dick was a freight line running on the Illinois Central Railroad. It has never made a run on the Norfolk Southern Line, which runs through Emporium PA.

*The Shaman Stone that Johanna uses is a replica of the red ocher handprints of women at the shrine of Ix Chel at Tulum in Mexico. Maya women who wished safe childbirth, the ability to conceive, or to receive medicine for the particular issues of women's health, petitioned the Goddess by dipping their hands in red ocher and leaving a handprint on the outer walls of the shrine. The Shaman Stone depicted is a real stone of power that was used in ceremony involving preserving laws that protect women's rights. It's creator graciously allowed its image to be used in this book. It is photographed with a sprig of cedar and sage, cleansing herbs used by woodland indigenous people and plains people.

The late night cookie raid actually happened at a prestigious spa hotel where the author once worked.

I started writing the chapter "Her One True Name" at four in the morning.As I wrote the final two lines in the chapter, the sun rose over the mountain. Dawn arrived with streamers of gray, orange, golden and pink lights.I did not plan it that way.It just happened.Ceremony is like that.

A special thank you to Skye Jones, an off-track thoroughbred racehorse rescuer and re-trainer, for graciously allowing me to include the real life Merlin's magical personality in this book. He is a million dollar racehorse who got a second life as a show jumper.

Anneka Lowrie writes the Johanna Kincaid Mysteries—psychological suspense stories drawn from real-world crimes, human behavior, and ancestral insight, delivered through twisty, high-stakes investigations. In addition to writing mystery thrillers, Anneka Lowrie is a retired psychotherapist who worked with victims of violent crime. Her Johanna Kincaid novels draw on professional insight into trauma, ethics, and the consequences of silence.

A Convergence of Crows was selected as a Quarterfinalist in the Booklife Critics Prize for the Mystery & Thriller category.

Anneka's Website

https://annekalowrie.com/

Join her Substack for behind the scene commentary, book trailers and character chats

https://substack.com/@annekalowrie

Subscribe to her mailing list:

https://bit.ly/FollowAnneka

Scan me

Clouds Over Katahdin

Book Two of the Johanna Kincaid Psychological Mystery Series

Available Now at Major Retailers

A psychological mystery where danger moves beneath the surface—and trust can turn without warning. When psychologist Johanna Kincaid travels to northern Maine to help an old friend harvest her herbal tea garden, she expects a season of hard work and quiet reflection. Instead, she finds a pattern of sabotage. And it becomes clear that someone wants Norah Jordan-Minsky out of the way. Set against the unforgiving Maine wilderness, Johanna confronts a crime hidden beneath respectability and fear.

Read the Johanna Kincaid Mystery Series-character-driven psychological mysteries that blend real-world stakes with a subtle, grounded intuitive edge. Follow Anneka Lowrie @ **https://www.annekalowrie.com/**